RONNY ALLARD

THE UNDERTAKER DOWN UNDER
CONDEMNED

Ronny Allard
ronnyeallard@gmail.com
PO Box 9084, Harkaway Victoria 3806, Australia

First published in Australia 2022

Edited by Tanya Smith
Typeset by Nikki M Group
Cover design by Andrew Seymour

ISBN 978-0-645018-12-7 (print)
ISBN 978-0-645018-13-4 (ebook)

A catalogue record for this book is available from the National Library of Australia

Contents

Warning

Stories in this book involve graphic depictions of death, including by suicide. They begin with my perspective and recollections as an undertaker, then create fictional backstories about victims.

Note that the content in this book is for mature adults, and not for children. Those living with mental illness in particular should exercise caution. Those needing support can contact Lifeline on 13 11 14 or Beyond Blue on 1300 224 636.

Introduction

*"It is a frightening thought that man
also has a shadow side to him, consisting
not just of little weaknesses and foibles,
but of a positively demonic dynamism."*
CARL JUNG

After writing my first book, *The Undertaker Down Under*, I was both startled and amazed by how the process opened the floodgates of my mind to experiences I had suppressed. I find it incredible how the human mind knows when to suppress episodic memories, storing them in a locked box in the shadows, deep inside the hippocampus of the brain. The consciousness of my memories stays hidden, only to be exposed when one of my senses betrays me. Triggered by a smell, a sight, a word, a touch or a foul taste, a still-frame of a recollection is unlocked. Like a hot flash in a pan, a memory becomes visible for a moment of a fateful day.

This second book delves into the dark side of humanity that we hear about from time to time. Carl Jung was a Swiss psychiatrist and psychoanalyst, well known for analysing the shadow part of humanity in what is now classified as Jungian psychology. His teachings explain that the shadow hides in plain sight of our ego consciousness. The conscious ego does not identify with the shadow until we are placed in certain conditions; for example, physical environments such as prisons, concentration camps or civil unrest. It can happen at any point in our lives, especially when we are faced with our darkest moments. At these moments, we have a choice: let the shadow overtake us, or turn away from it. And, when faced with the most significant test, some people let the shadow engage their consciousness to reveal their darker side, while others, having mastered the skill to control their shadow's dark impulses, can walk away.

The infamous Stanford Prison Experiment was conducted in August 1971 by Dr Philip G. Zimbardo. The study had volunteers participating in a mock prison held in a converted basement. Some of the participants were assigned to be prison guards and everyone else played the part of inmates. The experiment, conducted to observe and study the psychological differences between the prisoners and the prison guards, was to last two weeks.

The experiment lasted only six days before being halted abruptly. The study was discontinued as the participants instinctively embraced sadistic and authoritarian behaviours. The guards developed Machiavellian personalities in their new roles. The prisoners were subjected to psychological torture at the hands of the guards, and rebelled by barricading themselves in their cells using their beds, and going on a hunger strike. Zimbardo recorded that one prisoner, #8612, had started to act uncontrollably, displaying behaviours such as screaming, cursing and wild rage. The results of the experiment would seem to confirm Jung: the 'shadow of humanity' is universal – not something particular to individuals. Circumstance also plays a significant role.

As destructive as the shadow can be, it is also a vast pool of creativity. Throughout history, creators have harnessed and expressed the dark side in compelling and breathtaking art, theatre and literature, often underscored or influenced by culture and religion. This requires a fearless exploration of the dark waters in the depths of the deep caves of one's conscience. Most people are too afraid to scratch the crusty scab of Pandora's box and potentially expose this latent darkness.

Popular culture has commonly addressed this darkness in comedy or through art. A comedian approaching a taboo subject can get a laugh when tapping into a real insight that shocks and awes an audience. When the dark side of humanity is exposed and formulated into a joke, it can have a ripple effect through the collective consciousness, and the natural instinct and reaction is to laugh in the comfort of others. As the aphorism goes, *"If you want to tell people the truth, you'd better make them laugh, or they'll kill you."*

Comedians cleverly compose jokes based on what many are thinking but are too afraid to say.

The stories in this book are not formulated for humour. Instead, they take you on a journey where the shadows of humanity wreak havoc on everyday people. They expose the dark side of humanity that most people do not see regularly. Each chapter is inspired by my own experiences and those of my colleagues. It is a creative journey through the horrific scenes we witnessed all too often in our role as undertakers.

Each story starts with actual recollections: the sights, sounds, raw emotions, and people – alive and dead. These spill over into fictional imaginings of the backstory to the scene, drawing on available information and the insights of the undertakers involved, while maintaining the privacy of all.

Although an undertaker is not privy to all the facts, in most cases, we were given some insight into what had occurred in the lead-up to the event. In some rare cases, the attending police officers already knew the perpetrator before rigor mortis in the victim had taken effect. However, in most cases, substantial investigation was needed.

Mark Twain once said: "Growing old is a privilege denied to many." It's a quote I like to share with people when they complain about getting older or having a birthday. I've seen many people denied the chance to age. Every year is a blessing. Through reading these stories, I hope you will gain this perspective and embrace and enjoy the privilege of life.

Mile High Club

"Before you embark on a journey
of revenge, dig two graves."
CONFUCIUS

It is said that when our brains and hormones go wild due to someone else's presence, we go into a state of limerence, a feeling of obsession and infatuation for that person. This intense obsession can be motivated by anything to do with that person: a smell, a look, their personality, a touch. In rare cases, the state of limerence can turn into a fatal attraction.

When I first embarked on my journey as an undertaker, my main concern was coping in an environment imbued by death. I was introduced to my co-workers, Jackson, Todd and Jay, on my first morning at the funeral home. After the initial greetings and jovial chit-chat, they began to share stories of what they had encountered when called out to a job. It felt as if they were ushering me into their inner circle, like a form of initiation to a secret club. After a while of listening attentively I asked, 'What is the worse scene you have encountered?' I would later find out for myself what it was like to step into a scene from a horror movie, to feel the hairs on the back of my neck stand upright, to see blood, to look upon disembodied remains, and to smell death – a smell that never leaves you. As soon as my question had escaped my mouth, a silence fell, and a blue undertone encompassed us. Jackson and Todd exchanged a look in complete silence with wide eyes. Todd broke the silence in a soft tone.

'The one we did last week,' he said, with eyes lowered.

Jackson nodded slowly and quietly responded with a quick, 'Yep'.

THE SCENE OF THE CRIME

Jackson and Todd received a text with an address that sent them across rolling stretches of barren farmland. As they drove away from the city in the undertakers' transit van, with its dark tinted windows and accommodation for up to five bodies, the warmth of the sun was melting away the last of the morning dew. Rounding a bend on a slight rise, they were confronted with the flashing lights of emergency vehicles. When approaching such scenes, your mind is bombarded with questions: *What has happened? Is it an accident, a crime scene, a suicide, a heart attack? How many bodies are there? What is the state of the body or bodies? Will we be here for hours?* These questions swirl around your mind until you take the first step into the scene. Answers then appear one by one, only to be replaced with more questions.

As the undertakers pulled up, a policeman approached their van and instructed them to be extremely careful when disembarking and moving around. As soon as they placed their feet on the ground, they could see why. A shallow impact crater was not too far from the car, an indent no one wants to see on a parachute landing zone. They knew someone must have hit the ground at high impact because the parachute that was supposed to slow the person down was lying on the ground, unopened. Jackson and Todd pulled on their rubber gloves.

The undertakers' task of removing the body from the scene can be difficult: crossing scrub bushland to cut down a man hanging from a noose in a tree, or picking up hundreds of pieces of human flesh strewn across a railway track. Or consider the task of detaching a decomposing 200 kg person from an armchair, whose skin and flesh separate on contact. At some scenes, the task of removing a body is like solving a riddle or logic puzzle: working out the best, and least disturbing, way of performing the task.

The accident site Jackson and Todd were confronted with that day was like looking inside a meat grinder at the end of a butcher's shift. Body parts were scattered across the large empty field like confetti. Larger body parts were easily identifiable, but many smaller pieces sat scattered on the top of the blades of grass and overgrown weeds still glimmering with dew droplets.

Jackson and Todd made their way to the impact crater. As they surveyed the area, in disbelief they saw the person's femur protruding vertically from the ground. At that moment, they ceased being spectators and began the task of removing the body – all of it. They stepped into the small crater and, with nothing more than the protruding bone to grip, they both cupped two hands around the bone and pulled. No luck. They adjusted their grip and tried again, this time pulling at a different angle. Still no movement. Wearing rubber gloves, their grip was not strong enough to dislodge the bone from its resting place. With each failed attempt, the bone began to resemble the legend of King Arthur's sword, Excalibur, lodged in stone, awaiting the right person to pry it free. Glancing at their torn rubber gloves, split between their fingers, they knew a different tactic had to be employed. At that moment, one of the police officers pulled a jemmy from the boot of a police car and handed it to Todd.

'Use this,' in an unorthodox tone.

Using the jemmy to dig and pry around the bone, Jackson and Todd finally felt some movement. They jimmied the bone free from its resting place. Everyone watching moved in at once to peer into the hole left by the leg bone, gasping collectively in disbelief at how far the bone had penetrated the ground. Assessing the depth of the indentation, the investigators surmised the skydiver had hit the ground head first, possibly intending to make a quick exit.

As Jackson and Todd gathered what was left of the man, they discovered more information about the accident, who the man was, and the circumstances which led to his death. They overheard a police officer talking about collecting enough evidence to convict those responsible. This was not the site of an accident; this was clearly intentional – and not on the deceased man's behalf.

After hearing the whole story, I was not only afraid to ever skydive, but I was also breathless to think this could have been anyone. A million thoughts flooded my mind about what could have been going through this man's head when he realised his parachute was not going to open.

THE BACKSTORY

Boyd was working his usual Saturday shift at the local timber yard. He looked at his watch for the umpteenth time as he waited for the last hour to go by. Only a few customers were strolling around, and most of the preparations to close up were complete. Another worker, Joel, was also waiting for the final hour to tick by, so he strolled over to Boyd. They began talking about their plans for the next day, which was predicted to be an extraordinarily hot day for late spring. Boyd mentioned that he would be catching up with some friends for afternoon drinks and a barbeque, then asked Joel about his plans.

'I'm going skydiving in the morning,' Joel said.

'Skydiving!' Boyd exclaimed, surprised. Boyd thought of Joel as a quiet but collected guy, confident and smart and always good to have a pleasant conversation with. Never would he have taken Joel for a skydiver.

'Is it your first time?' Boyd asked.

'No, I've been jumping for just over a year,' Joel replied. 'My friends gave me a birthday voucher a couple of years ago. After my first jump, I decided I wanted to join up. I have been doing it ever since.'

'Wow! That's frickin' amazing, man. I've never met anyone who skydives before.' Boyd's excitement was hard to hide. 'What's it like? Do you still get scared? Are you ever worried that your parachute won't open?' Boyd's mind buzzed with so many questions and the hour that felt like it was never going to end was now almost over.

'No,' Joel replied. 'It's not scary, and you learn to pack your own parachute, so you know it's done right.' Joel was trying to answer all of Boyd's questions, but then thought to ask, 'Why don't you come along in the morning and watch me do a jump?'

'Really? Yeah, sure! That would be awesome. Does it cost much to jump?' Boyd queried.

'Not if you sign up as a member; it works out a lot cheaper than paying each time as a non-member.' Joel closed the front gate of the timber yard behind the last of the customers. 'I'm sure you'll love it.'

Boyd headed home, excitedly thinking about the next day and the possibility of doing a jump at some stage in the near future. He wondered if this could be a regular thing. It wasn't like he was doing much in his spare time, and hanging out with a bunch of guys who seem to have no fear, would be an adventure in itself. He could already picture in his mind deploying the parachute, looking out over the views and to the distant ground below.

The following morning, Boyd arrived at the airfield and was greeted by Joel, with his trademark friendly smile.

'I'm glad you made it, bud,' Joel said enthusiastically. 'I'm about to jump. Why don't you come onto the field and watch from behind the fence?' Joel was already suited up in his jumping gear, and a group were walking towards the small plane out on the strip.

Boyd watched with childlike excitement as the light plane screamed up the runway and floated into the vacant blue sky. Other planes landed majestically, their landing wheels kissing the ground as they came to a rolling stop. Boyd thought back to a childhood memory of going to the airport with his dad and siblings when he was young to watch the planes land and take off. He had always had a fascination with aircraft and found them magical to watch.

At first, Boyd couldn't make out Joel's figure in the early morning light as each skydiver jumped out of the plane in perfect synchronisation. Boyd held his breath as he nervously hoped for each parachute to open. And sure enough, right on cue, the skydivers pulled their cord, and colourful canvases filled the sky like blossoming flowers.

Joel's brightly coloured suit came into view as the wide canopies glided through the air, bringing each skydiver safely to the ground. They then unclipped, got to their feet, wrapped up their parachute and made their way back to the hangar. Noticing the ease of each person's movements, Boyd could tell that these were experienced divers. Joel came over to Boyd.

'How do you feel about a tandem jump today?' Joel asked.

'Really?' Boyd responded, his eyes wide with amazement. He didn't know if he could mentally prepare himself in time.

'I was talking to one of the instructors, and he said he has some free time. Since you're a friend of mine, he's happy to take you up today if you would like to give it a try.' Joel's smile was even wider than before. He continued, 'It's on the house! Come on.'

In no time at all, Boyd was fitted with a harness and strapped inside a light aircraft.

'Ready to go?' he heard the pilot call back. Boyd could feel his heart beating hard inside his chest. Not only was this to be Boyd's first time parachuting, he had never been in a light aircraft before. The nerves set in, but the excitement of the adventure outweighed his trepidation. He also knew that the crew had done this a hundred times before and was confident they knew what they were doing. And, although he felt vulnerable, he trusted the people on that plane with his life.

As the aircraft engine revved loudly, the pilot manoeuvred the aircraft on a dime around to point its nose towards the end of the runway. Then, quite suddenly, it began to accelerate towards the end of the runway, picking up speed, faster and faster as the engine grew louder. Boyd could not help but look out the windows at the airfield and the surrounding paddocks as the plane became airborne. The sight was breathtaking: the neatly ploughed fields, the road snaking around the fenced paddocks. Then, as the plane reached the desired altitude, it levelled off with a few bumps, banked to the left like a fighter jet and headed away from the airfield. A short moment after the plane levelled off, someone up the front yelled out instructions, and the side door opened. Boyd expected to be more afraid at the thought of jumping out of the plane, but he found he was actually looking forward to falling with the instructor attached to him. As they edged closer to the opening, he could see directly under the plane's wing, and a second later, they were freefalling. The cold air rushed past Boyd's face like a leaf blower. The adrenaline zoomed through his entire body as time stood still. As the horizon began to rise around them, the instructor tapped him on the shoulder and then, with a jolt, the parachute deployed. Boyd was relaxed and enjoyed the views as they floated towards the ground.

After that first jump, Boyd was hooked and signed up to become a member. Over the next year, Boyd made many jumps, moving quickly from tandems to solo. He became part of the social group at the club and made many friends along the way. It was about this time that Boyd met Chelsea. The pair struck a chord and began dating. Chelsea had recently ended a long-term relationship with one of the other guys at the club. She was excited to put it behind her and move on with Boyd. She assured Boyd that she was well over the past. The relationship had been toxic and her ex-partner, Daniel, had been overprotective and jealous. Chelsea said the final straw was when she put on a miniskirt to go out to lunch with some girlfriends. Daniel went into a rage, put his fist through a wall and became abusive towards her. She packed her bags that day and moved out.

Boyd and Chelsea had been dating for a few months when the skydiving club held its annual end-of-year social night. It was a big moment for Boyd and Chelsea: their first social outing with the skydiving club as a couple. It was an opportunity to meet up with friends and have a good time. When they arrived, barbeques were lined up outside the hangar, accompanied by with the aroma of cooking sausages, burgers, and steaks. Coloured lights hung from the many steel beams, and music played in the background. The air was warm, the atmosphere was buzzing with laughter, and people were sharing stories of the year gone by. They knew it was going to be a fun night.

Boyd and Chelsea walked in and quickly embraced the fun. During the evening, Boyd noticed Daniel staring in his direction with a disturbing look in his eyes, like a

Bengal tiger in tall grass, stalking its prey. Boyd looked away and mentioned it to Chelsea. Chelsea brushed it off, saying that Daniel was just jealous. She knew Daniel still had feelings for her but, as far as she was concerned, it was none of his business who she dated or what she did. The past was better left in the past. Soon after, Daniel left and was not seen again for the rest of the night.

The following morning, Boyd arrived at the hangar for his now-regular Sunday morning jump. His usual crew and buddies had arrived earlier to prepare. The morning was eerily silent, with the sun just peeking through the mist; it was going to be a hot summer day. Boyd, noticing this silence and lack of wind, had an uneasy feeling that he couldn't place. He wondered if he was still coming down from the buzz of the night before. There was something about the way the chill of the morning mist caressed his skin that gave him a strong intuition not to jump. Everyone strapped on their gear and headed towards the awaiting plane. Boyd just couldn't shake this uneasy feeling, so he told the guys he would sit this one out.

'Late night, fellas. Just don't feel like jumping today,' he said.

'No probs,' replied one of the guys. 'See ya back on the ground!'

As Boyd walked back to the hangar, he crossed paths with Joel, who had arrived late and was running to catch the plane.

'Hey, Boyd, where ya going?' Joel called.

'I just don't feel like jumping today,' Boyd said.

'C'mon, mate! Let's do this. It's been ages since we made a jump together.'

Boyd reconsidered his decision and thought, *Yeah, why not?* He did a 180-degree turn and ran with Joel to the idling plane. A minute later, the plane was lifting into the clear blue sky.

By now, Boyd knew the sequence of a jump well: each movement of the plane, the position in which it levelled off, the moment the instruction came to open the doors. The uneasy feeling Boyd had about the jump made him hesitate for a moment, but with one almighty summoning of peace and courage, Boyd leapt out of the open door at 13,000 feet.

The sky was a lighter blue than usual, and the cool air engulfed him. Boyd took it all in while freefalling the first 1000 feet. The divers began performing flips and turns before manoeuvring into the 'iron cross' position. Boyd attempted a backslide: a freefall with his back towards the ground. Two other divers did the same. The three then performed the 'horny gorilla': connecting their feet and beating their chests. It was nice to share a laugh in the clear vacant sky. As they entered the 6000-feet zone, all divers broke away in preparation to deploy their pilot chute. This brings out the 'bridal', which acts as an anchor to slow the descent, followed by the main parachute opening at about 5000 feet.

Boyd reached for the handle tucked behind him to open his pilot parachute. The handle came away in his hand. He looked at it in disbelief: it had been cut, disconnecting it from the chute. He grabbed at the spare deployment handle on his right chest: the emergency backup for this exact scenario. As he pulled, time stood still, and the world stopped spinning. He gazed at the clean cut through the rope. As a tsunami of fear flooded his mind, he quickly reached for the RSL, the reserve static line, on the left side of his chest. This deploys the reserve parachute. Boyd prayed for an absolute miracle, hoping God or someone was listening from beyond the clouds. To Boyd's disbelief, it also came away. By now, the other divers were scattered far and wide, at different heights, underneath their colourful mushrooms. No one was close enough to be of assistance.

The dark realisation that there was no other option, no other backup, engulfed Boyd's whole body. His parachute had obviously been tampered with and was not going to open. Boyd knew in that split moment who did it. He felt foolish for not seeing it coming. He wanted to kick himself for not checking his pack more thoroughly – he had only given it a passing glance. He felt explosive rage, but also beyond rage: it was not an emotion he could afford to waste time on.

As a profound sadness welled up inside, he knew he had mere seconds before meeting his fate. In his training, he learnt that it takes approximately 5 to 6 seconds to freefall 1000 feet, and he was already only 4000 feet from the ground. All his options had run out. Like the last few grains of sand in an hourglass, Boyd could see his fate rapidly approaching. He looked for a soft landing. He could see the bay in the distance, but it was too far to reach at his speed and height. There were some trees behind the hangar, but he didn't have the skills to move that far in such a short amount of time. He could see no viable possibility but to pray for a miracle. The thought of his parents learning of his death was overwhelming. He prayed, *Even if I have to spend a year or two in hospital, God, please let me live.*

As he reached about 1500 feet, he concluded there was no surviving this. Boyd made peace with himself and realised the only control he had was over how quickly he would die. He knew that diving head-first could increase his terminal velocity to up to 280 km/h and that landing on his head would end things quickly. He didn't want to feel any pain. So, after making the last decision he would ever make in his short life, he moved into a dive and sped up towards the ground like a bullet. The last he saw were the white wildflowers of the bindweed on the grassy knoll, which he had noticed on his first flight lifting off the tarmac. Then, eternal darkness.

Mail-Order Bride

*"I thought about how there are two types
of secrets: the kind you want to keep in,
and the kind you don't dare to let out."*
ALLY CARTER

Jordan Peterson is among the world's most eccentric psychologists. Among many things, he talks about virtuousness, and how good men who are harmless and claim to be virtuous are nothing more than harmless men. Men who are capable of utter destruction and inclined to be dangerous but who choose to be *good men* are truly virtuous. The real monsters among us are those with no self-control and who cause utter destruction. Now and again we hear about men like this, and their deadly deeds make us shake with fear.

Can evil be rated, and if it can, should the number of deaths or the details of the deaths be the indicator of evil? At one end of the spectrum, there are the outright dangerous men we all know from history lessons: Mao, Hitler, Stalin, Pol Pot. These men oversaw the death of millions in some of the largest and most gruesome genocides of the past century. But also, on the scale of evil, you will find men and women throughout history whom we do not hear about until it's too late. They are living among us – hiding in plain sight. Some have regular jobs, a wife, a family: Josef Fritzl, Harold Shipman, Ted Bundy, John Wayne Gasy. These are just some examples of a dark entity lurking in the shadows of humanity.

A common characteristic of serial killers and the like is that they view their victims in a different light. To justify their actions, they class their victims in the same category as vermin, viewing them as less-worthy species, rather than fellow humans. When these criminals arrive at trial, they justify their deeds. Maybe they are more comfortable in the shadows than in the light.

This chapter shows how evil can live next door, unbeknown to many – even those closest. It begs the question: *how safe are we?*

THE SCENE OF THE CRIME

The undertakers I worked with described this scene as an eerie sight. The street was littered with police cars, detectives and bystanders when they arrived. This usually indicates someone has died under suspicious circumstances. When the undertakers get a call to a site, one or maybe two bodies require collection, and it is often an accident or murder-suicide. The undertakers knew this case was more sinister as they felt a thick ambience linger in the air. They pulled into the main driveway, a position always reserved for the undertaker's van, and unloaded a trolley from the back. As they approached the front door of the house, a police officer briefed them on the grim situation – multiple bodies in the backyard had been unearthed, and more may be found. The officer's eyes gave it away: there was no doubt something heinous had happened – a case that would almost certainly make the evening news.

The undertakers were led into the house by the police officer. Immediately inside was a long hallway. The first door to their right opened onto a TV room with an old brown leather sofa and lounge chairs symmetrically placed in front of a square box television in a wooden cabinet. The windows to the room were open, and the thick floral drapes danced about, letting in streaks of afternoon sunlight. The undertakers continued down the hallway, pushing their trolley over the plastic hall runner. They glanced at photos hung with care as they passed: photos of grown children and grandchildren, happy family portraits with everyone dressed in their Sunday best, and old school photos slightly yellowed from age. Police officers and detectives in suits, hurrying around like a swarm of European wasps, stepped aside to let the trolley pass. The undertakers were then directed through an old flywire door leading to the back garden, where more detectives and police officers were at work, busily gathering evidence. In the far corner of the garden was a large mound of earth and turned over plants, and just in front of the mound lay three bodies covered by bright blue tarps. The scene looked like an excavated cemetery.

One of the police officers stated the obvious: they would require multiple body bags. As the undertakers laid out the body bags in order and removed the blue tarps, the yard transformed to resemble a body farm you might see on a documentary. The three small-framed bodies were at different stages of decomposition. The first looked like it had been buried for years, nothing but a skeleton wrapped in some torn, deteriorating cloth, more at home in an Egyptian museum than a suburban backyard. Another body had decomposed so much that the flesh had wrapped itself around the bones and mummified – it resembled a frozen iceman who had fallen into a crevice. The third body was still decomposing: its fluids had drained away, and maggots were feeding on the remains. The skin had turned black like the frost-bitten toe of a mountain climber.

The undertakers placed the bodies into the body bags one by one and trolleyed them to the van through the side gate as discreetly as possible. Bystanders watched every move in disbelief from their front yards. This was their street, where their children played until sunset ushered them inside. These were their neighbours whom they had waved to when backing out of their driveways. The people watching must have felt a mix of emotions when they realised a mass murderer may have lived just doors away. When the undertakers went back inside the house to formalise the paperwork, the police officers disclosed how investigations into missing women linked to a dating site had led to this gruesome scene in the middle of suburbia, in the backyard of a retired couple's residence.

THE BACKSTORY

George had immigrated from northern Italy many years ago to escape the Mafia-ruled society. As a young man contemplating starting a family, he believed Italian life as he saw it was not what he wanted for himself and his future family. His opinion was that you're either in the Mafia or you're a victim of it. He decided to be neither, instead opting to start a new life in a new country with his new wife.

After landing in Australia, he found a job in a car manufacturing company and started working on the factory floor. His attention to detail and work ethic caught his bosses' attention, and he moved up to a managerial role. George did not disappoint, and ran his department like clockwork. Some would say he ran his department with an iron fist and a calculator. Although he was sometimes seen as an oddball, he was well-respected among staff and always got the job done.

To his surprise, when he arrived at work on his 60th birthday he discovered a cake had been organised to celebrate. This day also marked the 30th anniversary of his first day of work at the company. He was taken aback by how quickly 30 years had passed, and reflected on all the changes he had seen within the company in that time. He knew now was also a time of rapid change in the car industry, and the company was trying to adapt. Cars were no longer made like they were in the past: parts were cheaper to import than to make on the factory floor, automotive robots assembled the cars, and fewer people on the factory floor meant fewer people required to oversee operations. That afternoon, George received a call to head to the main office.

At the long table in the main office sat the operations manager, Garry, and the company's director, Bill. Walking in, George had the sense he was being ambushed. He knew what was about to happen so he took a seat. The men told him that the company had been undergoing some transformations, and his department would become obsolete in a month. They gave him two choices: he could go back to working on the assembly line, something he hadn't done in years, or he could take a severance package. From the figures they provided, George calculated he would be able to pay off what was left on his mortgage and use the rest to see him through the next 20 years, if he lived frugally. He decided on the severance package. George packed up his working life, and everyone wished him well in retirement.

A few weeks later, George's wife passed him an envelope that had arrived that day in the mail. It was his severance package. Inside the envelope was a thank you letter, a document stating the finalised payment and a cheque. Immediately, he was confused – the amount of was drastically less than he had been promised. He called his former employer and asked for an explanation. They explained that the amount was correct, as all taxes had to be subtracted from the total amount. George was furious – he would be lucky to survive financially for the next ten years on this amount. His wife had stayed home for decades, raising their four children, so he had been the breadwinner.

After hearing of George's retirement, his friend, Frank, popped in for a drink. George was happy for the distraction, as he was still worked up from the phone call. Frank and George had been friends for many years. Frank had travelled over from Italy in search of a fresh start around the same time as George, and their children had grown up playing together. George grabbed a bottle of homemade grappa, and they headed out to the garage. They set up chairs by the open door around an old fold-out card table, where they had sat many times before, and settled in. The flicker from a cigarette lighter was a symbol for the conversation to begin.

George told Frank about his situation: how he thought he had at least 20 years to relax with the money from his severance pay, but how the payment was so much lower than expected. Frank sympathised then told George about their friend, Mario.

'It's too bad you're married,' Frank said. 'Mario recently met an Asian woman online, and she paid him $30,000 to come to Australia, marry and start a new life.'

'Really?' George said, surprised. Mario's wife had died a few years ago. He had not heard that he had remarried.

'Yeah, he has extra money and a younger wife to cook and clean,' Frank replied.

'Do you have to marry them?' queried George.

Frank explained, 'You have to live with them for them to get a visa to stay. These women are looking for love, a new life, a home.' Frank continued with a smirk, 'Although, given that Mario is an old fart, she's probably waiting to get a visa, divorce him and take him to the cleaners for all his money.'

'Ha! Vaffanculo!' George swore in Italian at Mario's foolishness. As George and Frank shared a full-belly laugh, a seed was planted in George's mind. George wondered if this could be the solution to his money problems.

After a long conversation, George and Frank called it a night. Later in bed, Mario's new wife and life replayed in George's mind. George began to think of his options. He concluded an Asian bride was not going to be as lucrative as it sounded: he was already married, and he had no plans to leave his wife. He had a restless night's sleep as ideas danced in his head.

Over the next few days, George could not stop thinking about how $30,000 was a lot of money, and how it would help his situation. He went online and browsed the website Frank had mentioned to see what it was about. *Could he do it? How could he do it? Should he do it?* He knew the thought of it was absurd. *Why am I even contemplating this?* He couldn't shake the idea; the money was too good to pass up. George decided to sign up for the website. He created a profile with the username Mr G, clicked that he was single and explained that his wife had recently died, and he was looking for love.

The following day started like any other: his wife cooked him breakfast, he washed it down with a cup of coffee, and then headed out to his prized garden. It was not unusual for him to spend the whole day out there now that he was retired. His wife would bring lunch outside and they would eat together on a pretty table in the shade of a large old gum tree. Today, however, he couldn't stop thinking about his profile: *Has anyone seen it? How many people have responded? I wonder what they look like?* He went inside and sat down at the computer. He told his wife he had to search for how to mend a water pipe. He logged on. Already, three women had responded. He took a liking to a girl named Kim, who looked very attractive in her profile photo. She had responded to George's profile, stating how handsome he looked and how she was very interested in Mr G.

George replied, and the online conversation began. They started to get to know each other, and the replies quickly became romantic and sexual. Soon enough, George found himself addicted to Kim's messages. He succumbed to the attention, the adrenaline and the excitement, and found himself constantly checking his profile. Whenever George checked the time, he would automatically make the time adjustment for where Kim lived. He made sure he was online when Kim was up, and said goodnight when she would be heading to bed. George's wife grew suspicious of his constant attention to the computer. He had learnt to quickly make up stories of something he was looking up, learning or needing, to reassure her nothing was up.

George found himself falling for Kim and realised Kim was just as captivated by him as he was by her. He couldn't remember the last time a woman had paid him this much attention. George had lost his sense of reality: this was just a fantasy, all based on false pretence. George decided to entertain the idea of asking Kim if she wanted to come and live with him in Australia. Kim said 'yes' immediately, telling him that she loved him. George explained that he could do the paperwork to gain a visa and that it would cost her $30,000 for her to stay in Australia. Without hesitation, Kim agreed. She had no trouble coming up with the money.

That night, George thought about the money and how he could use it to buy more time in his retirement. There was still one major problem: he wasn't willing to leave his wife of 40 years. George began to set out an elaborate plan, starting with Kim arriving in Australia, and her handing him $30,000, and ending in the disappearance of a body. As she was from a Third World country and a long way from home, he figured, no one would know if she went missing. And if they did, he was smart enough to cover all his tracks.

It didn't take long for Kim to book her one-way ticket and arrive in Australia. The night she arrived, George told his wife that he was going out for the night with some friends from work. He then drove to the airport.

On arrival, Kim ran towards George at the arrival gate and they embraced. She was so excited to meet him. Her broken English was quite good, and she chatted away as George picked up her bags and they headed out to the car. Kim's excitement and bubbly nature saw George question his plans, but he quickly reasserted to himself that he was ready to do what he had to do. On the drive, George asked Kim if she had the money agreed on. Kim pulled out $30,000 in cash and showed George. George smiled and continued to drive towards home. Just before his street, he turned left towards a new industrial estate under construction and pulled the car onto a dark street. He pulled over in the shadows and told Kim to wait a minute while he checked something in his car. As George opened the boot and called for her to step out of the car, Kim grew suspicious. Not fully understanding what was going on, she reluctantly opened the car door. George grabbed her arm and pulled her out onto the sidewalk. He revealed a carjack handle from behind his back. Kim didn't have a chance to register what was happening. George connected the carjack with her head in one quick, forceful hit, and she was knocked to the ground. She let out a sharp scream as she fell. She hit the ground like a rag doll, sending shivers up George's spine. He knew there was no going back now. He looked at Kim, waiting in anticipation for any signs of life. After a minute, she let out a groan and tried to raise her head. With no hesitation, George took another swing, this time with even more force. He heard a loud thump and crack as her head smashed into the guttering. Blood slowly seeped out and pooled in a thick puddle. George waited, holding his breath, before releasing a forceful sigh. When he was sure Kim was dead, he wrapped her body in a new sheet he had recently bought, so as not to arouse suspicion from his wife, and dragged her body into the boot of his car.

Having no remorse for what he had just done, George took a look at the cash and counted it, feeling like he'd just pulled off the best crime of the century. He headed home and reversed his car into the driveway, with Kim's lifeless body in the boot. He washed his hands under a garden tap before heading inside. He went straight to the shower and then climbed into bed next to his sleeping wife.

The following day started like any other: breakfast with his wife. As it was Thursday, she then got ready and headed out the door, to meet up with friends at the market. George took this opportunity to move the body. He backed the car into the garage, collected a shovel from the gardening shed and began to dig. He had chosen a spot in the back corner of the yard where he always threw the grass cuttings. An hour later he had a hole large enough for the body. He dragged the body out of the boot and through the side door of the garage, which led directly to the backyard. He placed the body into the hole and quickly filled it in with dirt. George knew that the worms and bugs would help decompose the body, and no one would ever know. *What a great spot to plant some roses*, George thought.

A few months passed, and George was enjoying his retired lifestyle, spending his days gardening and relaxing with his wife. The money was stashed in a box in the garage and opened by George on very few occasions. He had treated himself to a new wheelbarrow and had taken his wife out to a special restaurant on their anniversary. Occasionally, he watched the news in the evening and Crime Stoppers to see if anyone declared Kim a missing person. Nothing. As no one came knocking looking for answers, George was confident he had gotten away with the crime. Then George contemplated going online again.

George logged on again. Within half an hour of browsing, he met his next victim, a young woman called Sonya. This time, George was very organised. He knew what he wanted and didn't allow emotions to affect his perspective. He would send a message to Sonya just once a day so as not to raise the suspicions of his wife. Sonya was very upfront and told George she found him very interesting. George allowed the conversations to escalate quickly, so that Sonya fell in love with his online persona, Mr G. The pair began to build a relationship, and within a fortnight, George decided to ask Sonya to be his bride. For just $30,000, he would arrange for her to come to Australia. Sonya responded with excitement, 'Yes!' She borrowed money from her family, intending to pay it back once she was settled in Australia, and flew into the arms of an awaiting Mr G.

After picking her up from the airport, George went through the same routine. It had worked so well with Kim, he was confident it would work with Sonya. He had even pre-dug the hole this time, dragging Sonya's body in the cover of darkness from the boot to the back corner of the garden, so as not to waste time. The next day, George bought four fruit trees.

George felt content that his plan had worked. Feeling like a genius, he carefully placed another $30,000 into the box in the garage. He then sat back and waited to see if anyone suspected anything. No one knocked on the door, he saw nothing on the news, and each morning, his wife cooked him breakfast. Life was good. Little did he know that the victims' families were actively looking for them.

After a few weeks, George felt untouchable. He had found a way to make some quick cash, and no one was the wiser. Feeling like a kid in an amusement park on a roll, George decided to do it one last time to set him and his wife up for a long and happy time. He began to dream of a wonderful retirement without worry – maybe even a trip back to Italy to see his brother.

Mr G logged on. George felt the adrenaline rushing through his veins and pumping through his heart. It was like he was sitting in front of the ultimate pokies machine and betting big with a high chance of winning. He soon met Zhang Wei. Her profile picture was of a woman with jet-black hair and skin like sparkling diamonds. She was in a cute blue top and a short skirt at the beach. She said she was 22 years old. They began to get to know one another, and within a week, George asked Zhang Wei to come to Australia to take away his loneliness. But Zhang Wei hesitated.

'What's wrong?' asked George.

Zhang Wei explained that there had been girls from her area who had gone missing after flying to Australia. George froze and felt his body temperature rise. He could hear his heart beating hard and fast in his chest, like a distant drum playing in the background.

'What do you mean?' he asked, trying to find out as much information as possible to determine if anyone was aware of the fate of these women, or who was involved in bringing them to Australia.

Zhang Wei told George that the girls' families had not heard from their daughters since they had left. Feeling relieved that it was only the families that were concerned, and not the authorities, George assured her he was not dangerous and, only looking for a companion. Mr G and Zhang Wei continued to build a relationship online. At times, George tried to find out more about what Zhang Wei knew about the missing girls. Zhang Wei thought they were isolated cases, and that many girls could find love in Australia. She had friends who had sent photos home to their families of their new life and babies. Zhang Wei wanted to be one of the lucky girls to make a new life in a new country.

Over the next month, George groomed Zhang Wei into trusting him. George proposed, and Zhang Wei accepted. The flight to Australia and the $30,000 was organised. Zhang Wei arrived, Mr G met her at the airport, and Zhang Wei was never seen alive again.

A week later, Mr G logged on to find a message asking to speak to Zhang Wei. It was from Zhang Wei's sister. Zhang Wei had told her family that she would contact them when she arrived safely. Her sister informed George that they hadn't heard from Zhang Wei and her family were very concerned for her wellbeing. George immediately deleted his account in an attempt to erase any connection leading to him. He tried to convince himself that there was no link between him and Zhang Wei, but he had a bad feeling in the pit of his stomach that stuck around like an invisible glue. *I should have stopped at two,* he thought to himself.

A week passed and George kept himself busy in the garden. At night, he sat in his armchair and watched TV. He struggled to relax as his mind could not shake the image of the message from Zhang Wei's sister. He had a feeling that the darkness that embraced him was about to come knocking. Then one evening, the phone rang. George's wife answered and passed the receiver to George.

'Hello,' said George.

'Hello, is this George, also known as Mr G on the dating site Narya.com?' said a stern voice.

George froze like a hare caught in a spotlight in an open paddock. There was silence for a few seconds.

'Hello?' said the voice on the phone.

'Umm, yes,' George fumbled. 'I mean, yes, I'm still here. Sorry, what was that site again?' He attempted to act like he had no idea what the person was talking about.

'My name is Detective Ferguson from the International Missing Persons Unit, and I'm involved in an investigation. I asked if you were Mr G?'

'Yes, that was my name,' George replied. 'I no longer use that service. Anything I can help you with?' George tried to shrug off the question casually.

'Did you notice any suspicious activity while you were online?' asked Detective Ferguson.

'No, not at all. I'm married. I have never met anyone on that site in person,' George lied. He continued, 'I spoke to one, maybe two women online. As I said, I'm married, and I'm sorry I can't help you.' George's wife was cleaning up in the kitchen, so George spoke quietly.

'Okay, sorry to have disturbed your evening. If you recall anything, don't hesitate to contact me.' Detective Ferguson gave George his phone number.

George pretended to write down the number and then thanked Detective Ferguson before hanging up.

George's wife returned to the lounge room and inquired who was on the phone. George, looking deep in thought, mumbled that it was the wrong number.

George sat and stared at the TV, but he did not see the screen, and could not hear the sound. A half-filled glass of whisky was in his hand, resting on the arm of the chair. George looked like he had frozen in time. But inside, he was in turmoil. He felt like the walls were closing in on him – like there was not enough air in the world to fill his lungs.

George replayed all three scenarios in his mind. He was trying to examine each case: the body, the weapon, the username, the money. He thought he had been careful not to make traceable contact with each woman. *What did I miss? Have they found me? What should I do?*

George tried to reassure himself that he must be among thousands of users the police were contacting. He maintained confidence that he had outsmarted the authorities: *No one can prove I actually met the women, let alone killed them; the money was cash; they have no bodies or murder weapons.* George hoped his long life in Australia as a model citizen would make him look innocent. With these thoughts and reaching the bottom of his whisky glass, he felt more relaxed. He went off to bed.

In the hazy light of pre-dawn the following morning, George awoke to a commotion at the front door. He sat up, slipped his feet into his slippers and shuffled down the hallway towards the living area. His wife followed. Before George could say anything, a wave of blue uniforms stormed the area; police officers with guns drawn and bullet-proof vests on. George's self-assurance was knocked right out of him. He knew the game was up. One policeman forcefully took hold of George's arms and yanked them behind his back. 'You're under arrest. Place your hands behind your back and don't move,' the policeman said.

George turned around to see his wife standing behind him, looking afraid and confused, and beginning to cry in fear. The only words George had time to say were: 'I've always loved you, darling. I did this for us.' He was led out the front door just as the morning sun peaked over the horizon.

The Defacto

"Walking away from a toxic relationship takes significant courage, and is often the first step to respecting yourself."
RONNY ALLARD

Domestic violence is nothing but ugly. It is utterly destructive to everyone involved, from the victim to the person who hears the story on the 6 o'clock news. It's important to understand that victims of domestic violence are both women and men. It is a plague on our society, like a curse from hell itself.

Some time ago, I was at a wedding rehearsal in Tasmania. Also in the bridal party were two police officers, Lisa and Romeo. As we stood at the altar preparing for a wedding the following day, we began small talk about our jobs. On finding out that they were police officers, I asked about the most common crimes they encountered. Within seconds, they had both responded that it was domestic violence. This was not the answer I was expecting. I was prepared for answers such as home invasion, grand theft auto or drugs. If they had said grand theft auto, I would have questioned the most elaborate case and type of cars involved. If they had said drugs, I would have wanted the juicy details of drug lords and kingpins getting caught. Instead, I found myself caught off guard. In the years since this meeting, I have learnt of the extensive resources allocated to domestic violence.

I'm lucky to say that, growing up, I never experienced nor was I exposed to domestic violence. Unfortunately, for others, domestic violence was, or is, part of their everyday life. I can't imagine what it is like to be trapped like a prisoner in your own home, unable to escape as a predator guards your every move.

Those lucky enough not to have first-hand knowledge of domestic violence may question why people do not just leave a toxic relationship. This thought comes from a lack of understanding of the psychological control one person can have over another. The Stockholm Syndrome is a psychological response that can develop over weeks, months or even years. It is where a victim sympathises with their abuser and defends their actions. This can lead them to accept their situation, blame themselves for any abuse they suffer or return to an abusive relationship.

In the case I'm about to share with you, the victim summoned up the courage to leave her abusive partner. The former partner became so consumed with anger that the situation escalated to the abuser taking the victim's life. This case was particularly disturbing for all officers who heard the call on their radio that day. As we arrived at the scene to remove the body, we saw the hopeless devastation across their faces. The gravity of the situation weighed on their shoulders that day, while the images would have troubled their minds for years to come.

THE SCENE OF THE CRIME

Early one Saturday morning, I received a text to collect a body. I called my colleague to let him know I'd be there shortly to pick him up. The address led us to a popular inlet where the water stretches as far as the eye can see. The inlet is filled with wildlife and mangroves. In summer, fishermen line the ramp waiting to launch their boats into the water. Families fill the air with laughter, barbequing at the picnic area on the grassy knoll by the white sand.

I had been fishing there many times; a friend and I would sit on the pier for hours, sometimes in the moonlight, to escape the summer heat, with rods draped in the water, hoping to catch something. Truth be told, I didn't have much success as a fisherman; I wasn't the 10% that caught 90% of the fish.

As we pulled up to what would typically be a peaceful, picturesque scene, with the reflection of the morning sky shimmering off the still water, we saw police tape enclosing a section of the water's edge. A few police officers were pacing back and forth, searching through the lush vegetation. Crime investigators were piecing together evidence and taking photographs. Two officers were questioning an older couple who were helping them with their enquiries.

Our eyes locked with those of an officer walking towards us. As we met, he proceeded to give details of the body, its location and the circumstances surrounding the body. His voice quivered with a hint of terror as he warned us about what we were about to see. We knew we were at the scene of a gruesome crime.

By this time, another officer had joined us. She informed us that it was now okay for us to take the body away. She spoke to us in a soft, quiet tone. 'There's a body of a young woman that was pulled out of the water from among the mangroves. Prepare yourself; it is a disturbing sight. Please be as discreet as possible, so the residents don't see too much.' I turned around and could see people looking out from the balconies and driveways of the houses that lined the area. Word had spread quickly that their quiet neighbourhood was the site of a gruesome murder.

We returned to the van, put on white rubber gloves and pulled out the trolley from the back with a newly opened body bag. As we followed a police officer to the body, he pointed out an area of tangled mangroves on the water's edge where the body had been retrieved from. He explained that the young woman's body, now lying lifeless on solid ground, covered by a blue tarp, was discovered by early-morning walkers not long after sunrise.

As the tarp was lifted from the body, I froze in horror. There, on the sandy bank, lay the motionless body of a young lady who looked no more than 25 years of age. She had deep stab marks on her chest, throat and arms. White and yellow discharge oozed from the multiple puncture wounds at the top of her breasts. Her throat had been slit so deep that the cross-section of veins, arteries, windpipe and muscles were exposed. The sight was so shocking that I stumbled back a few steps and looked away for a moment just to fathom what I had just seen. Feelings of utter disgust and horror were quickly replaced with anger, which permeated every inch of my body. I distinctively remember hearing someone ask how evil a man would have to be to carry out this act of violence. *A man?* I thought, *This is no man; her life was taken by a beast roaming among us.* The attack on her body was akin to that of a wild animal.

I collected myself and assisted my partner in placing the victim's ice-cold body into a body bag. It was then that I noticed the bruises covering most of her body, along with more slashes on the whole length of both her forearms. It was evident that she had fought for her life. We carefully placed her into a body bag and onto the trolley before pushing the trolley up the embankment to the van. After loading the stretcher into the back with the victim's soaking, wet body neatly wrapped in the body bag, we drove to the nearest hospital, where a doctor certified the time of death and the cause of death. We then transferred her body to the coroner's.

The woman's death and some of the gruesome details were on the news that day. When footage from above the crime scene of investigators working at the taped-off site were shown, I found myself looking away. I realised I had reached my limit. Any footage I would see would only further ingrain the images in my mind of what I had witnessed. The young woman's cold, mutilated body defined evil; I knew a part of me had been scarred for life.

Later that evening, we were called out to collect a body not far from my home. The deceased was an older gentleman who had suffered a suspected heart attack. When we arrived, the man's wife was spending a few moments with her deceased husband, so we stood with the police officers in the kitchen. We spoke quietly among ourselves about what we had seen and heard that day about the gruesome murder of the young woman. A police officer revealed that many of the neighbours had heard the scuffles and screams, but thought wild animals were fighting in the distance. One resident had recalled she was close enough to hear a blood-curdling scream, followed by silence, so she did not go and check. She had just assumed some wild animals were fighting over something. I can understand why some people thought it was animals: at night, all the wildlife come out to feed on the lush vegetation. But to think someone was close enough to hear her cries only to ignore them was devastating. I could tell this shook the officers to the core as they reflected in hopelessness.

They looked like they were old enough to have children about the same age as the victim. Even though I did not have any children at the time, I still felt the gravity of the situation.

I later learnt that the former boyfriend was the one responsible for luring her into his car. He was apprehended the following day. It was bittersweet to know that the person behind the vulgar act was caught and would be spending many years in prison. Of course, this could not erase what had happened.

THE BACKSTORY

Asher was at the funeral of a close friend who had died in a skydiving incident. Later that evening, she went to the hangar with some friends for the wake and to lay some flowers in memory of their friend. While there, Asher met and began talking to Bryson. She thought he was striking: his strong jawline and messy long hair reminded her of a wolf in the wild. She felt comfortable talking to him and felt like time stood still as she looked into his eyes. They exchanged numbers and began texting each other.

Soon, they were dating. Asher enjoyed Bryson's quirky sense of humour and appreciated his mature view of the world around him. He seemed more responsible than other guys she had dated. He was paying off his own house and had a pet dog he adored. She fell in love with him, melting in his warm embrace.

A few months later, Asher moved in with Bryson, and they couldn't have been happier. Then, as the months rolled by, she began to see cracks appear in Bryson's seemingly casual nature and calm outlook. He showed signs of insecurity and insensitivity, and exhibited an irrational temper. At first, Asher made excuses for him and justified his reactions in her mind. But these reactions and incidences became more frequent and more disturbing. Bryson began making absurd accusations, accusing Asher of having affairs. He would run through the house looking in cupboards and under beds for men hiding in his home. He rummaged through her handbag and pockets of her jackets, looking for evidence of a betrayal. Asher knew there was something seriously wrong with Bryson. She realised that she did not feel safe anymore with him. By this point, they had been living together for about two years.

On a regular check-up, Asher confided in her doctor about her situation with Bryson. She explained some of the most recent events and told her doctor that she wanted to move out but was scared to do so. The doctor referred the matter to a psychiatric nurse and organised an appointment for Asher and Bryson to attend. The doctor explained that the meeting would be viewed from behind a reflective glass by a psychiatric team. Asher coerced Bryson to the appointment under the pretence that they were attending a couple's counselling session.

After speaking with them together, the doctor asked to talk to Bryson alone. Asher stepped out of the room, assuring Bryson she would be right outside. The doctor addressed the issue of Bryson's conviction that Asher was having an affair and the possibility of others living inside the house. Bryson went into a rage and elaborated on how Asher's affairs could not be proven but were real, and that things around the house were constantly being moved to other places and rearranged when they were asleep. Bryson's instabilities were evident, and the doctor signalled to the psychiatric team to come in. They concluded that Bryson was a threat to himself and had him admitted to a psychiatric ward for four weeks to evaluate his mental state.

Bryson went into a rage of uncontrollable anger and started looking for items to pick up and throw. Swiftly, Bryson was detained and led out the door. As he was being dragged, kicking and screaming, down the hallway, he shouted back at Asher.

'You set me up, you bitch!'

A few weeks later, Asher received a call to ask if she would be comfortable coming to the ward to talk with Bryson. The staff felt this might help him deal with some of his demons; he needed to know she cared for him. Asher agreed and a supervised meeting was arranged. The psychiatric team stood by as Asher and Bryson chatted. Asher assured Bryson that once his mental well-being was dealt with, they could return to the happiness they once shared. She assured him that this wouldn't come between their relationship. She let him know that she was taking care of the house and the dog while he was away. Bryson sat calmly while they talked.

Towards the end of Bryson's four-week evaluation, another meeting with Asher was arranged. The meeting started calmly, but then Bryson lashed out and blamed Asher for everything that had happened. He said he would never forgive her betrayal, and for what she had put him through. This frustrated Asher, given all the effort she had made to get Bryson the help he required. As Asher walked away, she decided that she and Bryson were over. It was time for her to move out and start a new life.

Bryson was released from the psychiatric ward the following week. On arriving home, he found the house empty of Asher and her belongings. A note was positioned on the kitchen table from Asher detailing why she had left and that Bryson's dog was at his parents' house. Bryson decided it was for the best and returned to his life before Asher had moved in. He was happy to have his dog back, which he had missed while locked up. Asher knew she had made the right decision. Her friends agreed, and they helped her move on.

A few months later, Asher was talking to her friend, Dannielle, about her whole ordeal when living with Bryson. Dannielle inquired whether they had bought the house together, or if Bryson already owned it when she moved in. Asher explained that he had bought the house eight years earlier. Dannielle was in her third year of law school and explained to Asher that she was entitled to half of the house's equity by law for the two years she and Bryson had lived in it as a de facto couple. Dannielle insisted it was the right thing to do and told Asher she would talk to the law firm she worked at about her situation. Asher would have been happy to walk away, but she had been thinking of buying her own house, and the extra money would help with the deposit.

Within a week, Asher received a letter from the law firm stating her case against Bryson and outlining the nature of the claim: she would be seeking 50% of the house's increase in value for the duration of residing in the dwelling. The letter was signed by a lawyer and witnessed by Dannielle. All Asher had to do was sign the attached acknowledgement, and the claim would be filed.

Asher was surprised at how easy this was and ecstatic she might have the money to buy a house soon. This initial happiness was soon replaced with concern when she thought of how Bryson would react. Her fears were justified. A few days after she returned the signed acknowledgement of the claim, Bryson called. Asher answered the phone. 'Hey, how are you?' she said.

'How am I?' Bryson replied 'HOW THE FUCK DO YOU THINK I AM?' he shouted.

'I have a letter here saying you're going to take half my house. A house I worked hard for and paid for!' Bryson continued angrily.

'Look, I'm only doing what I've been told I am entitled to.' Asher spoke in a soft, relaxed tone in an attempt to calm him down.

Bryson continued, 'This is my house. I paid all the bills and repayments; you merely lived here. You have no right to this house. It's mine. IT'S MINE, YOU HEAR?' With every word, Asher could feel Bryson becoming more and more unstable. She could not get a word in as Bryson vented. When he was done, he hung up angrily. At this point, Asher realised she had made a terrible mistake and wished she had not gotten lawyers involved. She should have let sleeping dogs lie, she thought to herself.

Asher decided to withdraw the claim and went into the law office to talk to Dannielle. Dannielle assured Asher that Bryson's reaction happens all the time in these types of cases.

'People are always angry when they receive the initial notification of proceedings, but they soon calm down. Bryson will understand that you are just seeking what is rightfully yours.' Asher left feeling she was doing the right thing.

A few weeks later, Bryson rang again. He told Asher he was sorry for his outburst and that he was angry when he received the letter.

'I've worked so hard to get this house, and I didn't expect to lose it so easily.'

'I'm not trying to take your house, Bryson. I am only claiming half of the amount the property rose in value for the two years I was there. I'm entitled to that,' Asher explained.

'Yeah, I know,' Bryson replied. 'Hey, the lawyers must be expensive, huh?' he continued.

Asher explained that they would deduct their payment from the claimed amount. She said she was not sure how much that would be.

'Probably a lot,' Bryson speculated. 'I tell you what, why don't we come to our own arrangement? We'll work out what's fair, and I'll pay you out. That will save you thousands in lawyer fees. You keep the money, and I'll make sure you're paid fairly.'

Asher hesitated. 'Umm, I don't know if it's a good idea. I've lost a lot of trust in you, Bryson.'

Bryson reassured her. 'How about we meet at the local shopping centre? There are lots of people around, and we can talk. See if we can come to a fair arrangement? You don't need to spend lots of money on lawyers.'

Asher agreed to meet Bryson after work at the food court of a large shopping centre the next day. She decided not to tell Dannielle anything yet. She would just wait and see if she and Bryson could come to an arrangement.

As Bryson walked up to the table Asher was sitting at, Asher was surprised at how well he looked. He was well-dressed and greeted her with a smile. He spoke calmly and had written down a few figures on a piece of paper. He explained that he would have a formal valuation of the house done by a real estate agent, and the exact increase in valuation would be calculated from that, but he had worked out some values from his council rates notices in the meantime. He showed her the figures. She was impressed with the effort Bryson had gone to. Asher felt the Bryson she knew when they first met was sitting in front of her. They chatted comfortably, and she liked the idea of saving thousands.

Asher said she would think about it. They walked out of the food court to the front of the shopping centre. There were still many people around. She said goodbye and started heading for the bus stop. 'Hey, I'll give you a lift home. It's on my way, remember?' Bryson joked.

She declined, 'No, I'm fine. The bus will be here shortly.' Bryson insisted he drive her home; it was the least he could do as it was getting dark. Asher knew it was another 20 minutes before the next bus would arrive, and if she took up Bryson's offer, she'd be home in 10 minutes.

'Oh, okay,' she said.

'Great. Follow me, my lady,' he smiled.

Not long after getting into the passenger seat of Bryson's car, Asher felt uneasy. This uneasiness escalated to fear when she realised they were not heading in the direction of her house.

'Where are we going?' she questioned Bryson nervously.

'I want to show you something. I saw something beautiful the other day and thought of you.' He smiled. 'It's not far. You'll love it.' Asher felt mildly reassured.

They drove for about 10 minutes as the sun set behind them. Bryson turned off towards the old fishing pier on the edge of the inlet the town had been built along. They had come down this way a few times when walking the dog.

'Jump out,' Bryson instructed Asher cheerfully. 'It's just over there.'

He pointed towards a small embankment on the edge of the water. Asher had always liked the mangrove trees that grew so peacefully on the water's edge, how their branches were reflected by the water. Asher got out of the car and waited for Bryson to join her. They walked towards the embankment. Then the peace of the mangroves was gone.

Bryson, without warning, pulled a knife from behind him and stabbed Asher in the back. In utter shock, Asher turned to run towards the houses, but Bryson grabbed her. Asher screamed and tried to fight off Bryson. He thrust the knife towards her torso over and over again as she held her arms up to protect her body. Bryson then punctured her chest several times. She turned and started to fall to the ground, but Bryson pulled her towards him and ran the knife across her throat, slicing it open. Asher gave a loud yelp before falling to the ground, gasping for air with every breath.

Asher knelt bleeding profusely from the neck in silence in the dim light from not-too-distant street lights. She knew any attempt to escape would be futile. She held both hands to her throat as blood gushed down her arms.

Bryson looked down at her with a smug expression. *That will teach you!* he thought. *You don't mess with me!*

He watched the blood drain from Asher's neck and was surprised she was still alive. Bryson thought she would have died by now. He couldn't stand and wait any longer in case someone drove past, so he took his knife one more time, flipped Asher over onto her back and cut deeply across her throat, slicing through the oesophagus. Bryson watched the life drain from Asher's body.

Feeling that the job was done and there was no movement detected, he dragged her body to the water's edge. He waded out until he was waist-deep and pushed Asher's body towards the open water, thinking the strong current would carry it out to sea. *Shark food,* he thought. *Too easy!* Bryson threw the knife into the water and drove home. His dog greeted him happily at the door.

The following day, Bryson turned on the news to hear that a body had been found by the water. *Oh no!* he thought. He was shocked to realise his plan hadn't worked. He went over everything in his head and admitted to himself that he should have checked the tides. Even so, he had been waist-deep in water; the body should have been carried away kilometres from where they found her. Feeling frustrated, Bryson tried to think fast. *What do I do?* Before he had time to take his next breath, Bryson heard a loud bang on the door.

'Open the door. It's the police.'

Knowing the game was up, Bryson lay on the ground and shouted back, 'I'm on the ground with my hands behind my back. Come in, ya fuckin' bastards.'

The police barged through the door and arrested Bryson.

After hearing the details of Asher's death and horrific injuries, a jury found Bryson guilty of first-degree murder. The magistrate handed down a sentence of life in prison. While sitting in prison, one question circled his mind, playing like a record in his head: *How the fuck did they know it was me? … How the fuck did they know it was me? … How the fuck did they know it was me?*

While in jail, Bryson received a letter from Asher's lawyers to say that the matter between him and Asher would be resolved. He was ordered to pay $20,000 dollars to compensate for the increase in property value for the duration Asher had lived in the dwelling.

Bryson scrunched up the letter and threw it towards the open toilet bowl, before collapsing onto a single bed in a cell miles away from everyone for the next 25 years.

The Butterfly Effect

*"Dream as if you'll live forever,
live as if you'll die today."*
JAMES DEAN

The call of adventure comes to us in different shapes and forms throughout our lives. Gaining a driver's licence is probably the most exciting accomplishment of any young person's life. It marks the beginning of real freedom and new journeys into a world unknown. It's a call to adventure for many who use this new freedom to explore and have experiences not possible before. Unfortunately, as we all know, this newfound freedom comes with a price. As Paulo Coelho said,

> *"Freedom has a high price, as high as that of slavery; the only difference is that you pay with pleasure and a smile, even when that smile is dimmed with tears."*

This newfound independence means taking on responsibilities that force us to make mature decisions and rational choices. These choices can be challenging while transitioning through adolescence. We are in unexplored territory, and wisdom is required to guide the journey of survival to adulthood. Wisdom is not cheap. The price we pay is mistakes, which we can learn from. This, in turn, reinforces and strengthens the neuronal connections in our brain. When faced with a new challenge, we can easily recall our past experiences to protect ourselves.

Most people who have the luxury of living through adolescence will have a story or two to tell of near-death experiences, when they or the people they were with pushed the boundaries to their limit. These stories bond people in a shared experience often recalled in great detail many years later.

Adolescence as a whole is like trying to walk safely through the streets of Acapulco, Mexico, for many of us. Acapulco is the most dangerous city in Mexico, if not the world, tainted with drugs, weapons, kidnappings and homicides. The dangers are due to a combination of factors: the prefrontal cortex of the brain – responsible for rational thinking and decision-making – is the last part to develop. Having a licence that allows a teenager to take control of a 1300-kilogram machine can bring about much joy ... or sadness.

In this chapter, I share an experience that made me reflect on my own stupidity growing up, and how lucky I was to avoid catastrophe. I feel fortunate to be here to share it with you. I hope young people who are new to driving will read this chapter and understand that the consequences of a moment of carelessness can have irreversible, long-lasting effects. It's not possible to make *all* the mistakes in one lifetime, but we can learn from others' mistakes and apply them to our own lives. This, in turn, can create small pockets of wisdom, which, hopefully, will be enough.

THE SCENE OF THE CRIME

The smell of fresh rain hitting the hot tarmac in mid-summer arrived moments before an unexpected deluge. The rainstorm swept into town and lasted only about ten minutes. It was a needed reprieve from the prolonged heatwave we were experiencing in the early 2000s. With days above 40°C and nights above 25°C for days, it was like living on the surface of the sun. Everyone's main concern was staying cool and getting a good night's sleep. No sooner than the rain had come than it evaporated off the scolding hot roads and pavements in wisps of hot steam. It was like mother nature was flirting with us as we all prayed and waited in desperation for some long-awaited cool weather to arrive.

Not long after a short-lived rainstorm swept through, I received a text to head to a location some distance from where I lived. I hopped in the car with the air-conditioner on high, and the radiating hot windows rolled up. It felt like I was about to drive on the surface of Mars in an LRV (Lunar Rover Vehicle). I drove to meet my partner before we jumped into the van to head out to the site.

An accident had occurred on a long stretch of coastal road surrounded by large banyan trees. These trees have giant roots, some as large as small trees, sticking out of the ground, hugging the tree as it supplies them with life. They would be more at home in an African savanna. We arrived and manoeuvred around the roadblocks, the scene littered with flashing lights and emergency vehicles. Police, crime investigators, SES volunteers and paramedics were scattered among the cars, all busy doing what they were trained to do.

We parked the van and disembarked. When arriving at a scene like this, it is hard not to be overwhelmed with everything going on. First, I scanned the scene to understand what we were dealing with. I saw a pile of concave metal that used to be an old Holden Kingswood sedan entangled in the giant roots of a large banyan tree. The tyre skid marks snaked their way behind the car and showed that the vehicle had left the road on the bend and travelled up onto the embankment, making deep muddy gorges in the grass, then hitting the tree at high speed. Next, my eyes focused on the emergency response personnel trying to free the metal wreck embedded around a tree. Not far from here, two paramedics were closing the back doors of an ambulance. I saw a single stretcher on the ground among the vehicles, with a motionless body partially covered with a white sheet. As there was no one around them, I assumed they were deceased.

A police officer emerged from the chaos and motioned for us to follow him. He explained the accident as he escorted us to the stretcher where a body of a young man lay. I'm taken aback by the sight. His body was intact but his head had been split open from the top of his skull to his jawline, exposing contents that resembled the spread, symmetrical wings of a butterfly. It was as if an axe had been driven in with a single motion, only stopping at the back of the skull.

I squatted down next to the body and assessed the injuries. Careful and respectful consideration has to be made to determine how to place a body into a body bag. As I knelt, I noticed a silence come over the scene, as if a volume dial was being turned slowly down, and all motion came to a standstill. Everyone was aware that the body was about to be moved, and this was their way of paying their respects.

I could feel all eyes on me as I looked at the body and tried to work out how to stabilise the head during transportation. Someone nearby suggested pushing the head together to prevent the brain from falling out. I placed one hand on either side of the deceased's head and brought the two halves together. Every seam came together perfectly, and it was at that moment I saw just how young the man had been. *What have you done to yourself?* I thought to myself. I reached for the sheet to wrap around the body but, to my dismay, the head slowly peeled open until it again represented butterfly wings. I don't know why I thought it would hold. It was apparent this was not going to be a one-person task, so my partner helped as we wrapped a cloth around to secure his head, then zipped up the body bag to transport the young man on the stretcher to the van.

I overheard someone say, 'It's unfortunate it rained while he was going around the bend after the dry weather we've had.' I considered the word *unfortunate*, paused and looked up. *Was the rain the cause of such a tragedy? Is mother nature to blame?* I don't think so.

We drove to the hospital in silence as we had many times before, trying to process what we had just seen. No music or radio, just the humming of the van's tyres rotating along the road. We knew what the other was thinking. Only when we found the right words to say would the silence be broken.

We would later learn that three other young men were in the car with the victim, all school kids from the local high school. They had escaped the wreckage with minor injuries and were taken to a nearby hospital.*

THE BACKSTORY

When Alfred immigrated to the country as a child, an error was made on his passport. His date of birth was recorded as 1979 instead of 1980, and this error was never corrected. This meant that on paper, he was a year

---

*Everyone who witnessed the scene that day would have a profound respect for the development of airbags. Airbags were made compulsory in new passenger cars in Australia in 2013.

older than he actually was. It was comical at first, like when he would claim to be the oldest in his class, but this *small* mistake would have disastrous consequences in the years to come.

Throughout secondary school, Alfred was somewhat in the middle of the hierarchy of kids in his school. He blended in among the crowd and went largely unnoticed. On his 17th birthday, he turned 18 'on paper', which was the legal age to attain a driver's licence. Alfred wasted no time in taking advantage of this. The weekend he passed his driving and written test, he was over the moon. His attention then turned to finding a car. Word spread at school that Alfred had his licence, one of the first in his class to have one. Suddenly, like lightning had struck, Alfred went from being unnoticed to being the most popular kid in his whole year level. While he basked in his newfound fame, there was still the problem of not having a car.

One afternoon, as Alfred stepped off the bus to begin the short walk home, he saw his mother walking towards him. She joined Alfred on his walk and asked how school was.

'Yeah, alright, I guess,' he replied. They walked towards home.

As they walked, Alfred's mum asked Alfred if he remembered Uncle Garry, his dad's brother. Alfred said he thought he did.

'Did he give me that fire truck as a kid?' Alfred asked. *That* fire truck was the only toy Alfred played with for two years. It was metal with rubber wheels, and Alfred would push it up and down mounds of dirt in the backyard, pretending to race towards imaginary burning houses and trees. Although it did not have a flashing light, Alfred loved how the metal felt like a real truck, not like his plastic cars and trucks. He could vaguely remember his uncle's face when he passed the truck to Alfred. Alfred hadn't seen him for many years, not since he was about five.

His mother replied, 'Yes, that's him. Well, I have to tell you that Uncle Garry died a few weeks ago.'

'Oh!' Alfred answered, unsure of the best way to respond. Alfred didn't really know Garry, but felt sad for his dad losing his brother.

'How did he die?' Alfred asked curiously.

'He has been a big drinker for years,' his mother said sadly. 'In the end, the complications from his alcoholism caused his death.'

'Oh!' Alfred responded. He now had an idea why he had not seen him in 12 years.

'Dad tried to stay in touch a bit, but they had lost contact in the last few years. Dad is sorting out his affairs,' Alfred's mum continued. 'He actually put you in his will.'

'Really?' Alfred said, his eyes opening wide. 'What did he leave me?' Alfred tried not to sound too excited, while wondering how rich his uncle was. He envisaged a man not too dissimilar to his father, dressed in a king's robe, with gold chains draped around his neck, standing in front of a large suburban house. He pictured thousands of dollars in his bank account, and how exciting it would be to show off his newfound wealth to his friends.

'His estate and assets will be sold, and Dad will get part of that. He left you his car.' Mum delivered the news to Alfred with a smile.

'A car!' Alfred exclaimed, no longer able to hold in his excitement. 'What kind of car? Where is it? When will it be here?'

'Slow down,' his mother laughed. 'Knowing your uncle, he was probably still driving around in the same car he's had forever. He lived as a recluse and never changed anything, but he loved that car.'

When Dad arrived home, he confirmed what Alfred's mother had said.

'I'll take you over to his house during the week, and we'll pick up the car,' his dad said. Alfred didn't press his dad to pick up the car sooner, as he knew how hard his dad had been working. His shifts at the power plant had been going late into the night as they tried to keep up with the increase in demand due to the heatwave.

The following day, Alfred excitedly told his friends about the car and how his uncle left it to him in his will. A reoccurring discussion point at school for the next few days between Alfred and his friends, Peter, Marcus and Zul, was where to go in the car. Mainly, they thought how great it would be to drive it down to the beach to escape the heat. Trips to the beach had been few and far between as they had to rely on an adult for transportation. *No more!* they thought.

Alfred struggled to concentrate on his school work as his mind kept drifting to daydreams of adventures in his own car. The day to pick up the car couldn't come soon enough. His dad arrived home early from work on Thursday to collect Alfred. They drove to collect the car, a 45-minute drive away. On the drive, Alfred asked about his uncle. His dad said he and his brother got along very well growing up and did everything together, but his brother's excessive drinking had driven a wedge through the family. He had tried to get him to seek the help he needed, but Garry wasn't interested. They hadn't seen or spoken to each other for a few years.

Alfred then inquired about the car, wanting to know what it was like. His dad started to recall stories of how much fun the two brothers had driving around as young lads in the new Holden Kingswood. His brother was two years older than he was, so he remembered sitting in the back of his father's car, with Garry in the passenger seat , as his father drove them to pick up the new car. His brother had been saving up for it for two years and was so excited that he had walked out of the office in the car yard waving the keys in the air. Alfred's dad smiled as he pictured the scene from so many years ago. He turned to Alfred.

'This car was Uncle Garry's pride and joy. You need to look after it.'

Alfred promised.

Alfred's dad turned off the main road and headed down some smaller streets. Alfred scanned the houses for the car his dad had described. Then, finally, his father slowed and swung into a long driveway. There, parked in front of the garage of a dilapidated old house, was a majestical beast of a car. It was a goldish brown Holden HJ Kingswood 1976. Alfred was overwhelmed by the sight and gazed at it like an astronaut looking back at Earth from space – it was absolutely beautiful.

As his dad brought the car to a stop, Alfred jumped out, his feet barely touching the ground. He ran over to the Kingswood, examining every detail with owl-like eyes. He could feel waves of excitement running through his whole body, with the hairs on his arms standing on ends. Alfred's eyes did not lift from the car, so didn't notice the rundown weatherboard house with a smashed window, or the shards of glass sprinkled on the overgrown front lawn on which the car rested.

Alfred's dad walked over to the Kingswood and ran his fingers along the width of the bonnet. He explained to Alfred that, when it was purchased, it was straight off the assembly line with all its original parts and, although the paint job could do with a touch-up, it was in pristine condition. He unlocked the car and slid into the driver's seat. The car revved to life as his dad turned the key in the ignition. He sat for a minute with his hands on the wheel. Alfred noticed his dad seemed to have a distant look about him, as if he were recalling fond memories from his youth. His dad returned to the present, jumped out, and popped the bonnet. He checked over the engine and then checked the oil and water. Alfred heard his dad mutter under his breath with a smirk, 'Good to see the old bastard kept up the maintenance after all these years.'

'All good,' he said to Alfred over the roar of the engine.

He threw Alfred the keys for their car parked behind them.

'I'll drive the Kingswood in front of you,' he said. Alfred couldn't hide his disappointment. He wanted to drive the Kingswood, not Dad's boring old car.

His dad noticed the look on Alfred's face. 'I want to make sure it's running alright before you get behind its wheel. I need to remember all its special quirks, so I can teach you how to drive it safely.'

On the way home, his dad drove painstakingly, and slower than usual. Alfred followed in agony, watching his car weave and dance through traffic, gliding between lanes, stopping and then accelerating with a sound like thunder at stop signs. By the time they reached home, Alfred couldn't wait any longer; he just wanted to slide onto the grey leather seats and get behind the large metal steering wheel. As soon as they pulled into the drive, Alfred jumped out and asked for the keys from his dad. His dad paused and then, holding the keys above Alfred's hand, said in a soft tone, 'You be sure you're careful.'

'Yes, Dad,' Alfred said as his dad dropped the keys into the palm of his hand.

'Just once around the block,' his dad instructed.

Alfred jumped into the warm driver's seat where his dad had been seconds earlier. He clicked the old-style metallic seatbelt into position and adjusted the mirrors. He then slipped the gearstick into reverse and carefully guided the Kingswood out of the driveway and onto the road. Next, he manoeuvred the gearstick into drive, squeezed the gas accelerator with his foot and sped off down the road. Soaking in the moment he'd been waiting his whole life for – freedom.

The steering wheel felt like he was driving a truck, and he could barely see over the bonnet. Driving this larger-than-life machine along familiar streets, Alfred looked at the empty passenger seat. He felt like he was breaking the law or something by being on his own. Soon that thought vanished – he was driving *his* car.

The following day, Alfred woke early. He called his friends and organised to pick them up and take them to school. That day, all the talk among his classmates was about how Alfred drove to school, like some rebel without a cause. Everyone wanted to see his new wheels, and Alfred showed the Kingswood off proudly. Alfred knew this was the beginning of his expanding popularity at school. Over lunch, Alfred and his friends organised to take the car for a spin down to the beach the following day.

On Saturday morning, Alfred's friends rode their bikes to Alfred's house and gathered around the car, laughing while waiting for Peter to arrive. Once Peter arrived, they piled into the Kingswood with their towels and headed out of town towards the coast. There were lots of cars heading the same way, as the mercury climbed into the high 30s. They wound the windows down and put their faces into the wind, their hair blowing everywhere. They felt like kings of the road, heading out to explore a brand-new world. With his friends in the car, Alfred pushed the pedal to the metal, showing off how fast the car could go. His friends cheered him on at every move. Feeling confident, Alfred turned down a back road, and proceeded to drive well above the speed limit, high on the adrenaline rush. Alfred slowed the car down as they entered the small coastal town and pulled the Kingswood into the car park outside a takeaway shop opposite the beach. The boys headed in to grab a bite to eat. As they were leaving the shop, a sudden rainstorm rolled in from nowhere. They scrambled to the car and sheltered inside while the rain pelted down on the roof. They could see the beachgoers scrambling up the sand dunes in a mad rush, looking for shelter. Others danced in the rain to relieve themselves from the summer heat. Soon after they had arrived, the storm dissipated, and the hot summer day returned. The clouds drifted off to the east, leaving behind a soggy mess. Steam rose from the asphalt in the hot car park.

The boys changed their minds about going straight to the beach and decided instead to take the car for a drive along the coastal roads. As Alfred pulled out of the car park, he found that the car's wheels spun on the wet roads. The boys in the car cheered as the car drifted sideways. Alfred laughed and turned sharply back onto the road to achieve the same drifting effect. The roads glistened in the sun with a mixture of water and oil. Feeling like a race car driver, Alfred allowed the car to drift sideways around a few corners, taking advantage of the wet roads. Once out in the open, on a long stretch of road with no more corners, Alfred decided to give the car a test drive, going faster than he had before.

'You drive like my grandma,' shouted Marcus.

'I would have been home by now,' Zul added with a laugh.

The trees on the road's edge wooshed past as Alfred kept his foot firmly on the accelerator, giving his friends the thrill of a lifetime. Not wholly seeing over the car bonnet, Alfred was late to notice a slight bend in the road that he wasn't anticipating. He tried to slow the car down a little, and as he took the turn, panic set in. He managed to control the vehicle, but it was still going at high speed when they exited the bend. Alfred held the wheel tight, trying not to run off the road. At the speed he was going, both sides of the road were a dark, elongated blur. By this point, he was trying to slow the car down, but couldn't press the brake down hard enough while perched high to see over the bonnet. He considered another bend up ahead and had a fraction of a second to respond. He swung the car to the right, which he thought was the direction of the road. As he turned, all four wheels bounced off the road. Deafening sounds of terror escaped from the boys' lungs as Alfred desperately tried to turn the steering wheel left back onto the road. It was to no prevail, as he felt the front wheels slide violently from under the car, gaining no traction on the wet grassy knoll. He realised he had lost all control of this beautiful machine. He watched in slow motion as the bonnet collided with a tree, wrapping the front of the car around it. Alfred's head flew like a catapult towards the steering wheel, and everything snapped into darkness.

The Will

*"As long as greed is stronger than compassion,
there will always be suffering."*
RUSTY ERIC

When I think about the seven deadly sins, I conclude that greed triumphs over them all. Throughout history, greed has washed across nations and caused utter destruction and devastations.

When thinking about greed, the second deadly sin, many people would think of those with an unfair advantage in terms of power, wealth and resources. They might envisage a rich businessman who has little regard for anyone else. Most people do not think of themselves as greedy, yet they sometimes feel entitled to have more than they do. A shaman was asked: *What is poison?* His response: *Anything beyond what we need is poison.*

There is a natural phenomenon called the '80–20 rule', also known as the Pareto Principle. I was fascinated to learn it exists in every part of life, including: sports, fashion, wealth, business and music. The Pareto Principle says that 80% of the outcome results from 20% of the cause; for example, 20% of the seeds in a garden will yield 80% of the crop or 20% of people will control 80% of the wealth. It can also exist in family units, where 20% of family members will have more than 80% of the wealth or possessions of the others. This may cause some friction; for example, if you're waiting to inherit the fortune you never had the chance to enjoy.

This story demonstrates precisely this: a sole grandson waiting to inherit a small fortune from his frail old grandmother who decides to hurry along the process.

Carl Jung says the roots of the shadow of humanity reach all the way down to hell. He is implying that the human species is capable of unimaginable evil. The shadows draw out evil and darkness and bring the devil himself to take over. When I first learned about the shadow, this story immediately came to mind.

The raw effect of the destruction I saw throughout my career was shocking. But this case went on to echo in my subconscious for many years. It transformed my definition of evil. It is one thing to hear or read about evil, but witnessing it takes a part of you, never to be replaced.

As this case shows, greed can be damaging, and it can also act as a very good motivator. We can use it to our advantage by allowing it to inspire and motivate us, like a coach on the sidelines. As a country, it can help spur economic growth or social outcomes, which can place us higher up in the hierarchy of society. But where there is greed, good and evil will always be present.

THE SCENE OF THE CRIME

No matter how dormant or dull a street is, an incident requiring emergency services and undertakers will bring it to life like a shopping strip in the days before Christmas. The lights, the sounds and the wide-eyed people bring a buzz – an eerie, ghostly buzz.

We turned the van into what would normally be a quiet, lifeless street. The bold number, 41, screwed to the letterbox indicated we had found the house we were looking for. Generally, the street name is all we need, as other emergency vehicles and police arrive before us. In this case, we knew we had arrived at the scene of a crime due to the presence of undercover police officers in neat, pressed shirts with gun holsters strapped to their waists, walking back and forth between the house and clean, new-model, unmarked police cars. My attention was immediately drawn to the black suitcases they were carrying. I had not seen them on a job before.

We entered through a squeaky flyscreen door and turned into a dark, dull lounge room, which looked like it was frozen in 1969. An officer came over to address us. He asked us to wait a few minutes before collecting the body, as they were just finishing up in the room. This piqued my curiosity further. *What has happened here? I thought. Who is the deceased? What has led to undercover police officers collecting evidence? What are we about to see?* Earlier in my time as an undertaker, this curiosity may have made my heart rate increase and butterflies migrate to my stomach, but I had hardened in the environment that was now my reality. Now, it was like my mind flicked a switch, and I became an amateur detective, trying to piece together the scene and evidence to work out what had happened.

I looked around the lounge room, observing the artefacts, trying to gather clues as to who lived in the house. Usually, the fridge holds the most clues. The fridge often contains reminders, certificates and stickers left by children or grandchildren. There might be photos, mostly of loved ones, or birthday invitations and postcards. I quickly ascertained that an older woman lived in the house from the neat shelves of little knick-knacks. Family photos hung on the wall, and the floral lounge suite was in perfect condition. I could see through to the kitchen, where tea towels had been placed neatly on the bench to dry. The windows were draped in floral green curtains from the '60s. The table was free of clutter. Everything had a place. It reminded me of the house of one of my childhood friends, Domenic. His parents were from Italy and the house was always immaculate. You could always smell something cooking.

I continued to browse my surroundings, my thoughts interrupted when an officer came in and instructed us to follow her. Being led through the house felt like a ghost tour in a heritage home. As we neared then entered the room, the musty smell of death got stronger and invaded our nostrils. The first thing I saw was a pair of distinctive feet shrouded by an old light blanket.

On the carpeted floor lay a couple of the heavy black suitcases I had seen earlier. They lay open, exposing their contents. In one, I could see brushes, surgical scissors, test tubes and a mixture of other objects, all placed in clear evidence bags. The other suitcase held cameras, accessories and all kinds of lenses, filed between polystyrene slots to protect them from damage. A detective took a few more photographs of the scene, then dissembled his equipment and neatly returned each piece to its designated slot in the suitcase. Once the space was cleared, we prepared the body bag and moved closer.

The deceased was a small-framed woman, possibly in her eighties, covered from head to toe in black and blue bruises. It is confronting to see such trauma inflicted on anyone, but even more disturbing to see the marks of such force on an old woman. I didn't know what had transpired, but I knew it had been terrible. I could feel the suffering and the terror ringing through her body like a church bell. My attention was drawn to her hands; they were enclosed in brown paper bags, strapped up at the wrist with electrical tape to secure them. This was unusual.

Before touching the body, we were informed by an officer that the coroner's office had been notified ahead of time of the case, and had given specific instructions for preparing the body for transportation to preserve all evidence. We were instructed not to move the bags off the deceased's hands, be especially careful with her battered and bruised head, and drive straight to the coroner's office. Up to this point, I had not been involved in a case where such specific instructions on how to transport a body were given, which made me aware of the seriousness of the situation.

As we lifted her frail body, weighing no more than 60 kilograms, onto the awaiting stretcher, my face was just inches away from the bruises and blood blisters on her face. It was like looking through a microscope at a new world, but this wasn't a fun day in science class. The trauma evident on her body disturbed my inner soul. *Who would do such a thing to someone so defenceless?* I questioned. *How empty and evil would someone have to be to commit such an act?*

As we wheeled the deceased from the house, my partner said to a nearby police officer, 'How could someone commit such a heinous act?'

The officer replied that the suspected perpetrator was already in custody. I was surprised that the long arm of the law was quick at hand. He elaborated that the person they had in custody was the victim's grandson, who, they assumed, was after his inheritance.

That day, everyone in the house must have felt the gravity of the crime and the evil required to commit it. Part of me had assumed the special bond we had with our grandmothers, forged in childhood, was unbreakable. The pain was personal.

THE BACKSTORY

Jamie was a typical, bubbly, inquisitive eight-year-old. An only child and spoilt rotten, he was the centre of his parents' universe. Jamie knew how special he was to his parents: he was their one and only 'miracle baby.' They could not give him the brothers and sisters he asked for at the top of his Christmas list every year.

Jamie's world changed not long after his 9th birthday. The day was embedded in Jamie's memory. It was a dull and rainy day. Jamie was building yet another LEGO creation, piling blocks high on the shaggy carpet of his bedroom as the rain pelted against his window. His dad called down the hallway for Jamie to come into the kitchen. Walking into the kitchen, he was upset to see his mum wiping tears from her eyes with a small handkerchief. Jamie could tell she was trying to be brave in front of him, but struggled to keep it together. His dad was standing near the kitchen bench with a small glass in his hand, with what Jamie thought looked like cat piss in it. His father sculled down the remaining contents of the glass and sat it on the bench next to a half-empty bottle of whiskey. Jamie was taken aback by how serious both his parents looked. His dad looked over at Jamie and then at his wife, and tried to find the words to say.

'Sit down, son. You're not in trouble.'

Jamie stood there motionless, not sure what to do.

His mother motioned for Jamie to sit on her lap. Jamie went to his mother, and she embraced him. As he was absorbing the hug, his mother instructed his dad in a trembling voice, 'Tell him, Joe.'

Jamie turned to his father and watched as he summoned the words. Jamie had not seen his father like this before. Here was a man who was never lost for words. He was jovial when his mates came over for drinks, and they would sit around for hours playing card games. He was quick to speak up and criticise the newsreader when watching the new, and always had time to sit and play with Jamie. To see his father struggling to speak was strange to Jamie.

'Jamie,' his father finally said in a trembling voice. 'Your mother isn't well. The doctors say she is very sick.'

'Oh,' Jamie responded sadly and looked up at his mum. 'When will you feel better?'

'She won't, buddy,' his dad answered. 'She's not going to get better.' Tears were now falling down his father's cheeks, and his mother started softly sobbing.

'What do you mean?' Jamie asked. He sensed the world around him slowing to a halt.

Jamie felt his mother's grip around him tighten. She then began to cry uncontrollably, no longer able to contain herself. She buried her head into Jamie's shoulders. With a breaking voice, his father continued. 'The doctors say she has six months to live, son, which means your mum is going to die from her illness at some point.'

Jamie's eyes began to swell up with tears as he tried to process what he had just been told. He mustered up the courage to ask one last question. He turned to his mum and, in a voice only just audible, he whispered, 'Mum, are you really dying?'

'I'm afraid so, Jamie,' she replied between sobs.

Jamie hugged his mother tighter, as if holding her close enough would reverse the news he struggled to comprehend. No longer able to compose himself, his father walked out through the back door and into the yard, where he broke down. He was trying to be strong for his family, but hiding his own pain was difficult.

From that moment, Jamie's fears of the bogeyman that lived under his bed or in the closet no longer bothered him. Instead, his nightmare began when he woke up each morning, with the sinking feeling that his reality was not just a bad dream.

That week, Jamie didn't want to go to school. He wanted to be with his mother as much as he could. Most days, they would play board games and laugh. He tried not to think about being the little boy without a mum, but like a stretched rubber band, his thoughts would spring back into mind. In the late afternoon, his mother would go to bed. Sometimes, Jamie could hear her quietly crying. Jamie always knew, but he pretended he couldn't hear her.

As the weeks and months rolled by, his mother slept for longer periods. Her body grew weak until she was no longer able to get out of bed. Jamie would sit and talk with her, even when she was too weak to talk back. She would listen and reach out her hand to touch his.

Until one day, just like the afternoon shadow creeps in before the darkness, her strength slowly faded, and she never woke again.

After the funeral, Jamie's dad began to drink more and more. His drinking made him take days off work. At first, his employers were understanding and covered his shifts, but as the weeks turned into months, the company decided they could no longer accommodate Joe's poor performance. Now unemployed, Joe's drinking went into overdrive. Jamie was spending more time at his grandmother's house than at home with his dad. The situation continued all through Jamie's adolescence. Jamie had to fend for himself more and more; skipping school became a regular thing, along with smoking with friends. He now had a life with no ramifications, as there were no adults to bring him back into line.

By the time Jamie reached his early twenties, his father's drinking had well and truly taken over his life, and his health had deteriorated. Years of alcohol abuse had damaged his pancreas and liver. A tingling sensation was a sign that diabetes was affecting the nerves in his legs and fingers. Unmanaged diabetes then affected his vision, until one day, he fell into a diabetic coma. As his engine couldn't go an extra mile, it gave in, and Joe died in his sleep.

Jamie, now a young man and alone in the world with no boundaries or discipline, took solace and comfort in his circle of friends, who fulfilled his basic human need for social contact while sharing a joint.

He spent his days hanging out at the shopping centre while living on whatever welfare he could get from the government.

One day, while they were smoking a joint, Carlos pulled out a small zip-lock bag from his pocket. Jamie could see small, uniform, square-cut pieces of paper through the plastic, like tiny postage stamps. They had different bright-coloured patterns on them, some with smiley faces and others with weird cartoon figures and designs. Carlos opened the bag and carefully handed a square to Jamie and each of the other friends they were smoking with.

'Try this,' he said.

Jamie accepted, asking, 'What is it?'

'LSD, but it's also known as acid,' Carlos replied. 'You'll forget all your worries with this trip,' he joked.

Jamie watched Carlos place a small square of paper onto his tongue. He did the same. He then continued to muck around and chat with his friends: he felt no immediate effect. Then, like a heavy fog creeping in slowly, he began to feel his head spinning. He noticed his hands looked like they were moving in slow motion; he was mesmerised by the sight. Fingers appeared. It was as if he had truly discovered them, for the first time. He was amazed how they just hung off his hands. The patterns of his fingerprints began to swirl around, jumping and leaping into the air. More patterns appeared, leaping from friends' shirts and blending with the swirls of his fingerprints.

Colours jumped, twisted and blended, and then beamed brighter and brighter, like a lighthouse beacon in the distance moving closer towards him. Jamie heard words being spoken, which transformed into physical waves of sound vibrating individual atoms. The waves filled the air like ripples in a still pond before smashing against the walls.

Time became irrelevant, and Jamie knew he was entering a new world, like that of *Alice in Wonderland*. He was sliding fast down the rabbit hole. In his drug-like state, he thought he had a profound understanding of the real world. Everything seemed to connect and make sense to him, for the first time since the days of playing LEGO in his room all those years ago. Somehow, he made it back to his room, still very much feeling the drugs in his system. He looked at a tree through the window, and understood and could see through the soil to the ends of its the root system. Its vibrant green leaves lit up like Christmas lights. Everything around him exposed itself, removing the veil of reality. Jamie fell into a deep sleep.

Upon waking the next day, Jamie immediately wanted to go back to the world he had discovered. He started smoking a joint, but it didn't fulfil this new craving. His love affair with LSD had begun, and was like no other.

Drugs started to play a large part in Jamie's life, just as alcohol did for his dad. Jamie used drugs to escape – to forget how useless he felt for not being able to save his mum or his dad. However, no amount of LSD ever gave him the same effect as his first time. In time, Jamie graduated to MDMH, an even more powerful drug. Jamie's conflicting worlds collided: he could no longer distinguish between the real world and the drug-induced version. When high on drugs, Jamie felt free to lose total control, while feeling in control at the same time. With its limits of space and time, Jamie felt like he was inside a cheap video game in the real world. The boundaries didn't allow him to explore, and he felt trapped like a fly on a window, trying to escape, only to be held back by an invisible force.

It didn't take long for Jamie's newfound habit to surpass the little money he had. Jamie and his friends had resorted to stealing from unlocked cars at the shops and taking whatever valuables they could pawn or trade for cash. Jamie knew this wasn't going to be sustainable. By now, Jamie was well-known to the police and had a rap sheet of low-level misdemeanours longer than he was tall.

Then one day, while sitting at the skate park alone, sober and without a penny to his name, he started yearning to return to the time when his world was whole: when he was eight years old. He wished to be embraced with a warm hug from his mum, and laugh and muck around with his dad. Although he knew he could not bring his parents back, he thought of his grandmother and the love she showed him when his world fell apart.

Jamie had not seen his grandmother for five years when he found himself at her front door. He vaguely remembered it from his childhood. This was as close to home as Jamie would get. He knocked twice on the red timber door and waited. His grandmother opened the door, her face transformed with a beaming smile as she recognised him. She unlocked the flywire, and he followed her inside to the lounge room. She motioned for him to take a seat and then walked through to the kitchen and flicked the kettle on. She reappeared with a tin of biscuits. Placing them in front of Jamie, she asked him what he'd been up to. Ashamed to tell the truth, Jamie lied that he'd been working odd jobs to pass the time.

While his grandmother rattled around in the kitchen, clanking cutlery as she made herself and Jamie a cup of tea, Jamie's eyes wandered over the shelves of small trinkets, some of which he had bought or made for his grandmother when he was young. He noticed how well-kept they were and free from dust, despite the years they had been there. Then Jamie noticed the furniture, and how well-kept the house was. He thought about his current living conditions and his destitute situation. It occurred to him that one day this house would be his. Jamie asked his grandmother how long she had lived in the house and if she owned it.

'I've been here all my married life,' she said from the kitchen. 'Your grandfather and I bought this house when we were first married.'

She continued, 'It was one of the first houses built in this neighbourhood, and we used to look out from the front deck onto parklands. Over the years, all these houses popped up. The place sure has changed.'

She re-entered the room and handed Jamie a plate with a sandwich filled with ham, cheese and a slice of tomato, and sat a cup of tea on the small table to his left. Looking down at his plate, Jamie couldn't remember the last time anyone had made him something to eat. Noticing the ham hanging off the side of the bread, he realised he couldn't even remember what ham tasted like.

His grandmother continued. 'When we first moved here, your grandfather worked in a sheet metal factory, which used to be on the corner where the petrol station is now down the road. I worked at a clothing shop once your mum was old enough to go to school. When we paid this house off, your granddad bought the factory and ran it for many years.'

Jamie's grandmother's eyes lit up as she recalled those early days. She said it was so nice to talk about them with Jamie. Jamie took a bite of the sandwich and inhaled in delight; it tasted so good in his empty stomach. He thought to himself he could get used to eating like this every day. He started thinking about the house again, and how one day he would end up owning it. His mind drifted to thinking about how much the house might be worth.

Jamie and his grandmother talked through the afternoon, then she suggested he stay over to get a good night's rest. Jamie explained that he had a place to stay, sharing a room at a friend's house. His grandmother insisted he stay a night or two. She could see how thin he had become and how tired he looked.

Jamie, thinking about his last hit of cocaine wrapped up in his back pocket, said he'd better get going, but his grandmother wouldn't take no for an answer. He agreed to stay the night. One night in the room he played in as a kid filled with old distant memories wouldn't be that bad.

As the night drew to a close, Jamie lay awake in his old bed with memories zig-zagging through his mind: playing on the rug, reading his favourite adventure book, his gran's home-cooked meals. It saddened him to see where he was now, who he had become. Jamie decided to snort up some of the cocaine to help relieve the sadness and make the night bearable. Without any sort of drug, he found it difficult to rest. As he snorted, his grandmother popped her head in the door to say goodnight, just as she would do when he'd stayed over many years earlier. He looked up like a deer caught in the headlights, not knowing what to do next. She saw what he was doing and swiftly made her disgust known.

'What are you doing!? Are you doing drugs in my house?' She then yelled, 'If you've got drugs, you can get out of here.'

She then directed the most hurtful comments she could say at Jamie. 'If your mother saw you now, she would turn in her grave in disgust.' She continued,

'You'll turn out just like your Dad, wasting your life away until you also fade into a worthless human being.'

The words hurt Jamie like nothing else, and the anger built in him. He didn't know what to do or say, so he grabbed his jacket and stormed out the front door.

As he walked towards his mate's house, his grandmother's insults began to boil up inside him. Each word penetrated like a blade, twisting to cause maximum damage. Jamie became inflamed with absolute rage. He recalled that rainy day, playing with LEGO on the shaggy green carpet. Knowing deep inside he had failed his parents and his grandmother, he punched the front wall of a shop as he passed, leaving a dent the size of his fist in the steel sheeting.

Jamie never felt as alone as he did that night, lying on an old mattress on the floor. He stared up at the slither of light on the dark ceiling, coming through from the gap where the curtains didn't quite meet. Jamie felt that not even his grandmother cared about him, the only family he had.

Over the next few days, Jamie stayed in bed in a depressive state, bemoaning his life. He had nothing; he was nothing. His mind wandered, including fantasising about the day his situation might change – when he would inherited his grandmother's home. He was still fuming from the hurtful words she so angrily yelled at him. Dark thoughts started to enter the haze inside his head – ideas of ways to fast-track his inheritance. The more he thought about it, the more he fantasised. He realised that all that was standing between him and his fortune was that bitter old woman.

An idea was born one night while he was in a drug-induced state. It became clear to him what he would do: make his grandmother's death look like an accident. That was the only way for him to access his inheritance and get what he felt so deserving and entitled to.

As Jamie sobered up the next day, the thought lingered and festered at the back of his mind. He began to hatch a plan to pull it off without being caught. He read up on murders and house break-ins and learnt how to carry out both. *She will die one day anyway; I'm just speeding it up*, he justified. *Who would give a second thought to an old woman dying in a house invasion gone wrong?*

He decided to go ahead with his plan. He would make sure it was a moonless night and sneak through the back door to make it look like a break-in.

After a couple of weeks of planning, Jamie found himself in the large backyard of his grandmother's house, surrounded by pot plants on a moonless summer night. It was completely silent and the air still warm as he used his pocket knife, his tool to cut up drugs, to carefully and silently pry open the back door. Surprised by how easy this was, he walked quietly and gently down the hallway to the door of his grandmother's bedroom. It was already ajar. Placing one foot carefully in front of the other, he snuck into the bedroom where his grandmother was sleeping, oblivious to the danger that lurked by her side. He paused at the sight of her under an old woollen blanket and contemplated walking away, thinking: *Walk away; no one would know I was here; I can't do this; what am I doing?* But greed had taken over and quickly shook all these thoughts from his mind.

He wanted this house, and he wanted money for drugs. He wanted the only reminder of his past life gone, so he would not have to be ashamed anymore of who he had become. He pulled out his pocketknife and held it up, ready to stab, but then quivered at the thought of blood spurting out – the sight of blood made his stomach churn. He decided to smother her face with a pillow. *This will make it look like she simply died in her sleep,* Jamie thought.

He moved slightly to reach for a pillow on a chair beside the bedside table, but as he did, his grandmother awoke. She looked at him with piercing, terrified eyes full of understanding. Jamie knew he was past the point of no return; he had to act and act fast.

Visibly shocked, Jamie's grandmother reached out and grabbed his shirt. As her fingernails scraped down the side of his ribs, Jamie panicked as shame gripped his whole body. He quickly looked around for a weapon. His eyes landed on an old walking stick leaning against the end of the bed. He grabbed it and spun it around so that he had the butt end directed at his grandmother. With one forceful blow, he connected with the side of her head. She let out a sharp screech in pain, which broke the silence of the darkness. Jamie was worried that the neighbours would hear her screams, so he silenced her with another strike to the head, more forceful than the last. Blood droplets sprinkled in the air like a fine red mist as she let out a shallow groan. He couldn't bear the sight of her blood-soaked face, so he pulled the sheet over her face to hide the shame of what he had done, like a creator repulsed by his creation. The memories and feelings of every misfortune that had happened to him came spilling out like lava from an erupting volcano. He unleashed blow after blow after blow with the solid wooden stick, first to her head and then to all parts of her body. It felt like he was watching someone else as his emotions vanished, and he allowed rage to take over. Everything that life had dealt him to this point – death, misfortune, abandonment – engulfed his whole body. He beat his grandmother until his arms lost all strength. He released the stick from his firm grip with white knuckles and dropped to his knees.

He didn't look at the bed to acknowledge what he had done. He didn't want to know if his grandmother was alive or dead. He just wanted to get out of there. He got to his feet and, without looking back, headed out the bedroom door. He stopped at the kitchen and went through her bag. He found a handful of notes and change. He threw the money on the floor to make it look like a robbery and left through the front door.

Jamie spent the next two days replaying the scene over and over in his mind. *Did I leave anything? Has someone found the body? Did anyone see me?* Although he felt this was a low point in his life, he had no remorse.

He was just worried that he would be caught, and if he did, what punishment he would receive. *Jail for sure,* he thought. Before the sun had replaced the darkness on the third day after the attack, Jamie was woken by dogs continually barking next door. Moments later, he heard the front door break down and shouting.

'This is the police!'

He jumped out of bed as officers stormed his room and jumped on him. It was game over.

Apples and Trees

"The apple doesn't fall far from the tree."
PROVERB

This chapter is less shocking than what's come before. Nevertheless, I remember how I felt when I heard of the connection between two fatalities on the same night, just hours apart. Everything seemed to stop as I tried to decipher what I had just heard. Like the afterglow of a death star, that feeling of astonishment has not been shaken from me, even years later. I hope this story highlights the dangers of drug addiction and how important it is to set an example for the people around us.

Addiction is often associated with alcohol and drugs because they cause more fatalities than any other type of addiction. While working as an undertaker, I witnessed whole families addicted to drugs and alcohol. It was always sad to see, as the likelihood of breaking the chain in cases like this is slim to non-existent. Drawing on personal experiences over many years from dealing with my sister's alcoholism, I know how tough the fight can be – trying everything in your power to save that person from themselves.

Amid trying to run a business and hold up my household with my partner, dealing with an alcoholic sister was stressful. I completely understand the struggle families go through, and I don't envy their situation. Fortunately, after many health scares and complications, my sister managed to turn her life around. After a decade of abuse, she now lives with permanent complications while trying to get her life back on track. Yet I'd say we are among the lucky ones – recovery is not the case for many.

In my first two books, I draw on my experience with my younger sister's addiction. With her permission, I share her experiences as a warning to others.

Experts have studied drugs for years, asking why people rely on them and investigating their long-term and social effects. Dr Bruce Alexander's experiments in the 1970s on rats became known as the 'Rat Park'. He wanted to see if drugs alone were the cause of addiction, or if social settings played a role. To test this, he placed rats in a large cage, free to roam, mate and play. He then isolated some of the rats to see what effect isolation would have on their mental state.

The isolated rats had access to two water bottles: one was laced with heroin or cocaine, and the other was plain water. Over time, the isolated rats went straight to the drug-laced water and kept drinking until their bodies could not take any more. In every case, the isolated rats overdosed and died.

Dr Alexander placed the same bottles in the enclosure where the rats were free to roam. These rats preferred plain water to drug-laced water. Occasionally, they would drink the drug-laced water, but only in moderation and never to the point of overdosing.

These experiments showed rats that were happy and had regular social interaction were less inclined to choose drugs to the point of overdosing. Dr Alexander drew on these findings to propose that when a supportive social network surrounds humans, they are also less inclined to use drugs in excess. Similarly, when people feel isolated, they may use drugs as a substitute for the pleasure they would otherwise they from a supportive social network.

While researching drugs to write this chapter, I gained even greater understanding of the gravity of addiction. As parents, we try to do everything in our power to steer our children away from the deathly shadows of drugs and alcohol. It would shatter my heart into a million pieces if one of my children had an addiction, and I was powerless to help them. I imagine this would be every parent's nightmare.

The following story is about a mother and daughter, who both dabbled in drug use, and how one night out went horribly wrong. It was shared with me by a colleague, gifted at building suspense within a story.

I hung on and listened silently, captivated like a boy scout sitting by the campfire listening to ghost stories.

If drugs and alcohol play a big part in your life, I hope this chapter resonates. What happened to this mother and daughter was devastating – especially as it was preventable.

THE SCENE OF THE CRIME

We pulled up at the funeral parlour after a long day transferring bodies to the coroner's office. I noticed the other van from the other crew was parked by the garage door. I was somewhat excited to see them, as this was the only chance we got to catch up, joke around and share what we'd been up to. Now, when a group of undertakers share what they have been up to, it will involve death, gore and smelly bodily fluids. It may seem morbid to an outsider, but this was our line of work. I mean, what else do a bunch of undertakers in the one room talk about? If a group of crows is called a 'murder', I dread to think what the collective noun for a group of undertakers is.

On this day, the guys from the other crew shared a story about a case where they were called to a popular nightclub in the middle of the city. They were led to a young woman in her early twenties, dressed to impress for a good night out with her friends. Unfortunately, she had not had the chance to impress anyone, as she had overdosed on drugs while still standing in line to get in.

She had started frothing at the mouth early in the night, and bystanders could not save her life. She passed away among friends.

On hearing this story, I thought that this occurrence, although sad, wasn't uncommon nor that interesting. But then they continued.

A few hours later, the undertakers received another text, this time directing them to a house in the suburbs. A woman had passed away alone in her home from a drug overdose. The undertakers arrived to retrieve the body, and when completing the paperwork, they realised that the woman had the same surname as the young girl they had picked up earlier in the city. Then they discovered the addresses of the women also matched. It turned out the woman and the girl were mother and daughter.

It seemed that the mother and daughter took the same drug, and both passed away on the same night, unaware of each other's death. The coincidence seemed like a sick joke, with the drug having the last laugh. Although it does not need mentioning how harmful drugs can be, the undertakers saw firsthand just what drugs can do to a family. It was goodbye for eternity for both of them.

THE BACKSTORY

Carlos emigrated from Columbia to live with his mother's distant cousin in the hope of building a better life. To make ends meet, he worked several jobs to sustain himself until he received his permanent residency. He did some printing and advertising online and helped his second cousin, Maria, with her part-time job cleaning high-rise apartments.

One night, Maria invited Carlos to come and party all night on the town with her and her friends. They were all in their mid twenties, enjoying life and carefree. While out, Carlos noticed the girls were queuing to buy something from a guy. Looking closer, he saw that the guy was selling pills. Carlos watched the organised chaos around him, and found it intriguing. Carlos was very impressed with the amount of money being exchanged. He wanted in; he wanted to be part of the deal.

Carlos made his way over and struck up a friendship with the guy, who said his name was Jay. Carlos summoned up the courage to ask Jay if he could help him sell some pills. Before long, Jay and Carlos were working as a team to sell pills at nightclubs spread across a large area. Carlos made more in one night than what he was earning at both part-time jobs combined. He made quick friends and quick cash. Soon enough, he was known to all the bouncers at the nightclubs, and to many patrons and revellers looking for a good night out. Carlos understood the risks involved, but felt there were plenty of people willing to tip him off if the police came through the front door.

Savannah was a friendly, bubbly character with a big heart. She was a regular customer of Carlos, and gave him a big hug with a broad smile whenever she saw him. She'd always get Carlos to supply her with a few *party pills* so she and her friends could dance like crazy until bouncers escorted them out at 6 am.

It was Carlos who had offered Savannah her first pill while outside a club. Without hesitation, Savannah accepted one and downed it like a Panadol. Her friends duplicated her move and then giggled and danced while they waited for the pill to take effect. As the tiny pill began to enter Savannah's bloodstream, it was like she had been lifted off the ground. Her body felt weightless. The deep, thumping bass of the music from inside the club vibrated throughout her body. She entered her own personal odyssey, with not a care for reality and its restrictions. Savannah and her friends were free to dance the night away, along the streets and into the early hours of the morning.

One day, Savannah called Carlos during the week, desperately seeking some pills for the long weekend. Savannah and her friends had been planning to hop between nightclubs. Not one to disappoint, Carlos agreed to meet Savannah to make the exchange.

After he hung up, Carlos realised he was dry: he had nothing in stock. Usually, he would have a few dozen pills in his secret stash, yet this week he was like a pub with no beer. He picked up the phone and rang Jay. The phone went unanswered. He tried again and again – no answer.

Umm, that's strange, thought Carlos.

Carlos sent a coded text to Jay, saying: *neighbours moved out. place vacant*

After a few long hours, there was still no reply from Jay. Carlos tried a couple more times, with no answer. Carlos began to worry, his mind racing. Finally, the phone rang. It was a friend of Jay's. He informed Carlos that Jay had been in a minor car accident, which the police attended. They found pills in his car and then raided his house.

God damn Jay, Carlos thought to himself, *Where will I get the pills now?*

With no time to waste, Carlos asked the voice on the other end of the line if he knew anyone who could fill his supply. The voice replied, 'You want car parts?'

'Yes, car parts,' replied Carlos. 'I can give you this guy's number,' said the voice, 'but you'll have to ask for car parts, and he'll know what you're talking about.'

Carlos rung the number and asked for car parts. Silence. 'Hello?' Carlos asked.

'Yeah, I've got some small car parts you can pick up.' A pick-up address was given, and the phone hung up.

Carlos headed towards the address as quickly as he could. Soon, he was turning off the bitumen road onto a dirt track and pulling up outside an old, white weatherboard house. A shiver ran down Carlos' spine as he stepped out of the car. This place could have been mistaken for a scrap yard or an abandoned house.

A tall, slim figure slowly strolled into view, emerging from around the side of the house in tattered overalls.

As the man drew closer, Carlos could see that the cracks of his hands were stained with oil and dirt, resembling a road map. *It looks like this guy was born under a car and stayed there*, thought Carlos.

Carlos got straight to the point. 'I was told I could get some car parts off you,' he said with a knowing look.

The tall figure looked deep into Carlos' eyes as if assessing his motives. With a nod, and an itch of his reddish-grey beard, the man replied. 'Yeah, that's right. What are you after?'

Carlos asked if he had the same pills as those Jay usually delivered.

'I don't know what the fuck you usually get, but whatever they are, mine are much better.'

Carlos followed the man to the shadows of the garage. The man showed him a bag of pills that looked almost identical to what he usually sold. Carlos decided to buy what the man was offering.

Carlos asked his new contact, who didn't give Carlos his name, if he could get more drugs if he needed them over the long weekend.

'Yeah, sure. Just yell out if you're low,' the contact said.

Carlos left, confident that his business was still alive and well. He met up with Savannah, offering her the acid or the pills.

'Just the pills,' Savannah said. 'Nothing stronger.'

Carlos forgot to inform Savannah that the pills were different to the ones he usually stocked.

Savannah and her mother shared a close bond. Savannah's mum, Sue, had been single since her husband left her when Savannah and her sister were young. Sue did have a lover, though, for a long time – her best friend's husband. Unfortunately, he died while they were making love one morning. Soon after, her best friend found out what had been happening between her now-deceased husband and Sue, and had stopped all communication. Then, Sue's other daughter, Savannah's sister, had moved interstate to marry some guy with money. That's when Sue turned to the occasional pill to overcome her loneliness. Savannah and Sue's relationship was unique, to say the least, as Savannah would supply her mother with drugs.

After meeting up with Carlos, Savannah arrived home and casually put the pills on the kitchen table in front of her mum. Savannah told her mum she would be out most of the weekend partying. Sue wasn't overly concerned for Savannah; Savannah was a big girl, and knew how to look after herself. Sue was a little disappointed, though, as it meant she would be home alone.

On Friday night, Savannah hopped out of the shower and spent an hour drying her hair. She then slipped into a new dress. Another hour was spent applying her make-up. She wanted to look extra special tonight. She was putting the final touches on when she heard the taxi honk from the driveway. She quickly grabbed her purse and chucked a few pills inside. Savannah gave her mum a quick hug as her mother uttered the words, 'Have fun and be careful.'

The taxi honked again. 'I will,' Savannah replied as she hurried out the door. The sound of the front door shutting behind her was like a starter's gun, marking the beginning of the adventure of a night on the town and the beginning of the long weekend.

Standing in line at a club with her friends, Savannah calculated that it would take about 10 minutes before they would get in. She decided to take out one pill from her purse. She then popped it on her tongue.

Within a minute, Savannah was surprised to feel light-headed. Her mouth began to dry up. Within another minute, Savannah was gasping for air. With every breath, she seemed to absorb less and less air. Her heart was beating rapidly, the thumping reverberating in her head. Her friends wondered what was going on, then saw she was frothing at the mouth. Panic set in, and they began to scream. This alerted bystanders, who ran over to help. But there was nothing they could do. Savannah was on the pavement, convulsing.

Carlos, standing in his usual spot about 20 metres from the club's entrance, saw the commotion unfold and realised what was happening. He slowly began to walk backwards away from the scene.

Death Race

*"True glory isn't found competing to win
against others. Competing against one's own
limitations and winning, that is true glory."*
RONNY ALLARD

Watching the hungry mechanical mouth of the jaws of life going to work at a car door and its hinges is a heavy reminder of how capability and can confidence work together hand in hand. Unfortunately, the scene we witnessed one day was proof of how the outcome can be deadly if the two are not balanced.

My introduction to capability and confidence wasn't long before the day I am about to describe.

I was sitting in a room with about ten other young guys, each of us eager to get a motorcycle licence. Waiting for the instructor, we chatted about our bikes. All but two or three of us were new to motorcycle riding, and we were all full of excitement.

The instructor came in, introduced himself and asked for a show of hands of those who had any experience on a motorcycle. Only a few hands were raised. Then, like a drill sergeant, he laid it all out on the table, looking each of us in the eye and delivering the painful truth – that motorcycle riders are 37 times more likely to die and nine times more likely to be injured in an accident than other motorists. He went on to say that more than half of us sitting in front of him would be in an accident, and three of us would die riding at some stage. At that point, you could see the horror in everyone's eyes. We all looked around, considering the statistic and trying to pick out which three of us it could be. It was at this point that the thought crossed my mind: *Am I doing the right thing?*

Everyone's dreams shattered. If he was trying to scare us, he was doing a great job. Then, shaking us up further, one of the guys who looked more confident and able to handle a bike than any of us stood up and left. We all watched in shock as he walked out. My conscience was screaming out to join him.

The instructor, Theo, waited as if to see if anyone else was going to leave, then continued his sermon on the importance of capability and confidence, and how the two have to be balanced. He explained that in riding, as in all parts of life, a balance was required to be safe. Having too much confidence and not enough capability can pose a hazard, and having very little confidence and a lot of capability is just as dangerous. This came as a surprise to me. It made me look at assessing all dangers in a different light.

Theo's words have been carved in my brain ever since. They have guided my love affair with motorcycles, like a safety harness. I don't know what happened to the other guys in the room that day – I hope they are still riding. If only the girl in the following story had been able to listen to his words of wisdom, she might still be here with us.

THE SCENE OF THE CRIME

One sunny Saturday afternoon, a text came through informing us that there had been a fatal accident in a nearby coastal town, not too far from where I lived. We drove out of town and joined the procession of cars, using the same route as many holiday seekers who were heading out to a nearby island. In ordinary circumstances it was a pleasant drive, but there was no pleasantry to what we were about to witness.

We pulled up to the scene. Cars were lined up for a few kilometres on the opposite side of the road. Traffic officers were directing traffic, but cars were moving slowly past the scene as drivers slowed down to get a good look at the carnage. Surrounding the median strip were police cars, emergency services, firefighters and a tow truck waiting to tow the vehicle once it was cut free.

We could see that the accident involved a car hitting a very large tree. The tree's trunk was wider than the car, and so tall that you had to tilt your head back to see the top. The car was a new model that had been released onto the market not long before. It was known to be a sporty, fast, small car full of punch. The car looked like it had hit the tree hard, as it was moulded around the trunk. The prehistoric-looking flaky bark had peeled away from the tree's trunk from the sheer impact of the car's bonnet and was hanging by threads on and around the vehicle.

We stepped out of the van and walked over to a group of police officers and emergency personnel, who were standing under the shade of the tree's canopy that towered us all. They were casually chatting among themselves while the firefighters were grouped around the car's wreckage, working away at trying to open the driver's side door. The car's rear end was just inches away from the road. As returning holidaymakers crept by in their cars, the only thing stopping them from seeing what was happening was a large blue tarp held up by a couple of emergency workers, which acted like a heavy curtain on a stage.

A police officer informed us that the woman killed in the accident was still in her car, and that the fire crew were trying to free her. We made our way to the mangled wreck of twisted metal, which just an hour earlier would have been cruising along this beautiful coastal road. We positioned the trolley near the car's rear and edged closer to look through the smashed windows. There, sitting in the driver's seat, was a young lady, her eyes shut, oblivious to the commotion of her new surroundings. Her mousy brown hair hung gently over her shoulders like silk, and her skin was pale, white and soft, like a single white cloud. Her head tilted gently to one side and her right arm rested on the door. Any given day, you would be forgiven for thinking she was asleep. I fought the strong urge to try to wake her from the a deep, lucid dream in which she appeared immersed. I had had this feeling before when I had come across other deceased people who looked like they were just asleep. At first, my mind would be flooded with thoughts for the paramedics to intervene: do something to get their heart started, give them oxygen, wake them up. Of course, my rational mind told me the paramedics had done everything they could before we had even been alerted. They could not change the outcome any more than they could change the rotation of the Earth.

By now, the other undertaker and I had joined the group of firefighters in trying to free the woman. I noticed that the whole front of the car was missing, engine and all. *It must have broken off on impact*, I thought. I quickly scanned the area, looking for the souped-up 1.8-litre engine, but it was nowhere to be seen. I observed that the twisted wreck, which resembled Picasso's painting *The Weeping Woman*, was hugging the tree in a tight embrace and the dashboard of the car was just millimetres away from the trunk, as if lightly kissing the tree. As I looked over the car door, I realised the car's engine had been ripped off the engine mount and had burst into the interior of the car. The engine had come to rest on her lap, leaving only a little room between her chest and the back of the engine, which now resembled a mechanical airbag. Her thighs were scorched red from the intense heat of the engine. It was painful to see. I knew what a delicate operation it was for the firefighters to free this young woman's body from the now cool engine on her lap.

Finally, the firefighters were able to push the car back far enough from the tree, which, in turn, repositioned the engine and released the woman's body. Once she was no longer pinned down, we were given the all-clear to remove her from the car. Just as we were about to do so, storm clouds swept in. I hadn't seen rain so heavy for quite a while. Our dry clothes absorbed every drop, hitting us like individual pinpricks as we placed the woman onto the trolley. Now, moving around like wet rats with motorists continuing to drive past slowly, watching our every move, we loaded the stretcher into the back of the van and shut the door. At that very moment, as if the door was a switch, the rain dissipated, and the sun shot rays from between the clouds. I don't know if her spirit was still with us, but it felt like she was trying to talk to us. We all observed the phenomenon of the rainstorm moving in just as she was being moved. *If she was communicating with us for the last time, what was she trying to say?* I wondered.

We hopped into the car in our soaked clothes and turned the heater on full. We attempted to dry our clothes before stopping at a nearby hospital to have her body certified by a doctor as legally dead. We pulled into the emergency bay of the hospital among the ambulances. We walked inside and let the clerk know who we were. She called for a doctor on her internal phone and we waited patiently. I spent this time observing the patients walking in and out of the emergency department and trying to guess what had befallen them.

A doctor came out dressed in a standard white jacket, clipboard in hand and a periscope around his neck. We led him to the van. The doctor's job is to determine if there are any signs of life. Sometimes, it's clear that a person is deceased; however, the doctors we encountered would follow procedure and listen for a heartbeat every time. Then, when they were satisfied that there was no chance the person was alive, they would issue a time of death and sign a form, a copy of which we would take to the coroner's office.

We drove the van into town to the coroner's office. As we drove into the coroner's office car park and stepped out of the van, the smell of death greeted us, as happened every time. *Couldn't they do something about the smell?* I thought as we offloaded the stretcher and wheeled it into an empty room. We handed the forms from the police officers and the doctors through a small window to the clerk behind the desk. Like a foreign exchange clerk at the bank, she processed the papers and sent out a technician with a glassy stainless-steel trolley to meet us in the empty room. The technician positioned his trolley next to ours, and we helped move the body. The stainless-steel trolleys have a drain plug at one end to allow blood and other fluids to flow down to a drain in the floor, leading to a special sump.

As the coroner removed all the young woman's clothing and placed her valuables in a bag for her loved ones to collect, he observed her body for any markings and documented what he saw. He then signed off the forms as we stood witness. As we left, he wheeled the young woman away into the other room to join all the other bodies.

THE BACKSTORY

All year, Dannielle had been studying for 40 to 50 hours a week in preparation for her bar exam. Most weekends, her head was buried in books, going over practice questions, scenarios and legal papers. It had been a vigorous, relentless year, but she was determined to reach her goal of becoming a lawyer, and that's what kept her going. But this weekend was different.

Waking up in between warm, soft bedsheets, Dannielle looked around the unfamiliar room. She recalled the previous night spent with her friends: laughing, drinking, crying. They had gone away for the weekend to spend time together after their friend, Asher, had been brutally murdered.

Staying at a beach house at the coast, Dannielle could hear the faint sound of waves crashing over the rocks in the distance. As she lay there, she tried to piece together how she had ended up in bed. The last memory she had of the night before was of being stretched across the couch, with everyone else scattered around the lounge room. Stories were being shared as they drank the night away.

Dannielle got out of bed and emerged from her room. She slowly shuffled into the kitchen, guided by the muffled chitter-chatter of friends who were already up. Walking past the lounge room, littered with emptied bottles and half-filled glasses on the coffee table, she could still hear the echo of last night's laughter and sorrowful cries. As she entered the kitchen, she realised the noise was coming from outside on the deck overlooking the surf beach. She walked out through the sliding door into the warm morning. As she sat down at the table with her friends, a wave of sadness again engulfed her. She remembered that Asher was not at the table. Usually the first one up, Asher was always full of energy and laughter. A sharp feeling of guilt travelled through Dannielle's body, so she cupped a warm coffee with both hands and looked out over the views that surrounded her.

Shortly after, Dannielle let her friends know she would have to leave as she had an exam to study for. An hour later, Dannielle was reversing out of the driveway. She started her journey home along the coastal road. Driving on an almost empty road, Dannielle reflected on the night. She was pleased she had taken a break from studying to spend some time with her friends. It had been a much-needed time together. Then, to her left, she saw another car similar to hers creep up alongside her. She glanced over her shoulder to see who was driving and noticed a couple of young guys looking in her direction. As they exchanged a look, the car beside her sped up. Never one to give in to a challenge, Dannielle also put her foot down and accelerated to catch up. Before she knew it, she was drag racing along the empty highway. Dannielle wanted to prove that it was not only boys who could drive fast. They exchanged taking the lead, their speed increasing each time. Dannielle's adrenalin was now freely flowing through her body, and she felt disconnected from herself and reality, yet at the same time fully connected to the machine she was controlling. The cars drove along the relatively straight road, with high cliffs to the left and the ocean's vastness to the right. With each second, they were edging closer to the dark shadowed corridor caused by a cluster of trees with towering canopies.

The cars raced into the shadows, with small slithers of light coming through the leaves. Dannielle's pupils opened up to try to adjust to let as much light in as possible. At breakneck speed, Dannielle lost sight of the road. Panic quickly set in. At this point, she didn't care who was winning. She realised what a dumb thing it was to take up the challenge. She lifted her foot off the accelerator in vain. Now the long road looked like a blur of thick tree trunks. Dannielle could not distinguish the trees from the bends in the road as her car was still travelling at the speed of a bullet. She felt the car vibrate and roar over the median strip. She turned the wheel sharply to avoid the tree trunks looming towards her. She let out a scream, silenced by the impact.

Skydivers with their deployed, colourful parachutes floated back down to Earth in the distance.

The Black Dog

"Every choice you make has an end result."
Zig Ziglar

The story I am about to share with you has been the most difficult to write. My hope is that you, as the reader, will gain a profound understanding of how the choices you make have a ripple effect on the people around you.

The chapter 'Peace Train', from my first book, *The Undertaker Down Under,* and this chapter both talk about how individuals succumbed to their depression. Writing both chapters brought back a flood of memories of a dear mentor and a good friend who met his end this way. This friend bestowed so much of his wisdom on me and gave me so much of his time that, without his presence, I knew I would be living in a completely different reality. Selfishly, I hadn't realised that while he gave so much of his time to ensure me and others were well looked-after, he had his own personal 'black dog' to fight. He silently wrestled with his depression and secretly made plans to exit this world. Learning of his death hit me like a ton of bricks. The music died, and silence took its place. His absence has been a constant reminder to me of our powerlessness to change the past.

If you are fighting battles alone, I hope you can find the courage to speak to someone. There are many services with highly trained staff who can help you in this area. I hope this chapter resonates with you and may help in some way to keep your black dog at bay.

Winston Churchill famously referred his depression as his 'black dog', coining the phrase. He was also aware of how powerful a split decision could be. In a letter to his doctor, he wrote:

> "I don't like standing near the edge of a platform
> when an express train is passing through. I like
> to stand back and, if possible, get a pillar between
> me and the train. I don't like to stand by the
> side of a ship and look down into the water.
> A second's action would end everything. A few
> drops of depression."

Churchill acknowledged how dark thoughts could creep in like a slow-moving storm cloud to cause utter devastation. He was willing to seek any form of help to rid himself of depressive thoughts after finding out a friend had successfully been treated for depression. In a letter to his wife, he wrote:

> *"I think this man might be useful to me – if my*
> *black dog returns. He seems quite away from me*
> *now – it is such a relief. All the colours come back*
> *into the picture."*

When I was a young man still in school, I remember being told a story about a man who was contemplating suicide. While talking to his psychiatrist, he realised how his actions and choices would affect many people for years to come, especially his loved ones.

His psychiatrist, who was worth his weight in salt, asked this man some tough questions after he confided that he was contemplating suicide.

'So, when would you plan this?' the psychiatrist asked.

The man replied, 'When the kids are at school, and I have the house to myself.'

'How would you do it?' the psychiatrist questioned.

'I'd shoot myself to make it quick,' the man replied.

'Hmm, interesting! So, tell me, who would find you first and so on?' asked the psychiatrist.

'Well, my son would come home first, then my daughter. Not long after, my wife would arrive and then the police.' The man slowly realised how his decision would affect his family.

The psychiatrist explored this realisation further, spacing the following questions out to give the man time to think about the ramifications.

'What effect would it have on your son finding his father in that way?

'How would that affect your son for the rest of his life?

How would your daughter and wife cope with your loss?'

The man realised how important he was and how his action in a split second would affect those around him for life. He thanked the psychiatrist and reassessed his view of life.

We may not be aware of it, or we may not like it, but, our choices have a profound effect. Some call it the 'butterfly effect': one action triggering an endless cascade of consequences.

A story I came across on the internet illustrated this beautifully for me. It is about a small, seemingly insignificant choice a man made in a moment, which, unbeknown to him, would have an enormous impact on his future, and indeed saved his life many years later. The story begins with a young boy reprimanded by a shopkeeper after being caught trying to steal something. After hearing the commotion, the man in the shop next door comes to investigate. He asks the young boy what he is accused of stealing. The man sees that the boy has a small bottle of medicine in his hands. The man makes a choice and offers to pay for the medicine for the boy.

Years later, the man is struck down with a potentially fatal illness. Without a lifesaving operation, he will surely die. As his daughter lies crying by her father's bedside in the hospital, she falls asleep. When she wakes later, there is a note in an envelope beside her addressed to her and her father. The note reads: '*The operation has been covered and fully paid for. Thank you for your help many years ago.*'

The note was signed by the surgeon. As it turned out, the surgeon was the small boy who was caught stealing medicine for his mother. He recognised the man and remembered the generosity the man had shown him that day. The surgeon then made a choice to repay the man's kindness.

We have all had moments in life where our mood is at its lowest. We may feel worthless and do not know how to pull ourselves out of the hole of despair. In a now famous speech in 2014, Admiral William H. McCraven talked about how the simple act of making your bed is a small and seemingly insignificant thing that has the power to turn everything around. The idea is that a small action done right will lead to another action and another until it compounds to form a more significant action that did not seem possible at first.

The same message was promoted by Jordan Peterson, who talks about how doing a minor task like cleaning your room can be the beginning of changes in the state you are in. These men are aware that a simple action that brings with it a tiny spark of accomplishment and worth can drastically change everything around you and, in turn, change your life for the better. What starts as a simple act has the power to change and influence you and the people around you.

If you find yourself in a rut, I would highly recommend performing a small action and doing it to the best of your ability. See what happens. As they would say in the military: *A bad plan is better than no plan at all.* The following story is about a man who decided to turn his rifle on himself in a decision that ended his life.

THE SCENE

When walking along a dark driveway to a front door, we never really know what we are about to see. Each case is like a mystery box. Sometimes, I wish we had known what we were walking into to ease our suspense. Would it have made it any easier? Probably not. On rare occasions, we were given some clues, such as the location. If the text said *train station*, we would assume someone had jumped or fallen in front of a train. If the text gave the location as a *bridge*, we knew we had a jumper. But when walking into a typical suburban house, we did not know what awaited us beyond the front door.

It was a dark evening when we were called out to the aforementioned typical suburban house. As the front door opened slowly, like in the house of mirrors at an amusement park of horror, we immediately saw a man sitting on a couch with his head tilted back. There was blood splattered all over the wall behind him, as well as on the curtains, the sofa, the ceiling. It looked like red confetti had been thrown all over the room, like the morning after New Year's Eve. But this had been no celebration.

While police officers moved around the room, the sound of the man's family in the kitchen, mumbling and mourning, filled the air. As soon as the paperwork was completed, we gathered the body bag and the stretcher and placed them by the door to make an easy exit. For the most part, the man looked like he had fallen asleep watching the Sunday games on the TV. With everyone moving around like the mechanisms in a fancy Swiss watch, the sense of urgency to move the body was thick in the air. I was busy formulating a plan to get a stretcher into this crowded, 10-foot by 10-foot room when I took a closer look at the body. It was then that I realised the top of the man's head was missing. As we stared down at his skull, like a cracked-open, bloody coconut, the officers filled in the gaps. They explained that the man had shot himself with his rifle. As I scanned the room for the rifle, I saw it resting against a couch with its tip pointing towards the roof.

After carefully moving his delicate body into the body bag, we retrieved a few zip-lock bags from the back of the van to begin the arduous task of finding and bagging the remainder of his skull. The high-powered bullet had scattered large and small chunks of brain and skull in all directions.

Up to this point, I had always thought that when someone shot themselves through the mouth, the back of the head splattered outwards in a neat streak in a uniform direction. I had possibly gained this idea from how it is portrayed in the movies. I remember thinking at the time, *How could Hollywood get it so wrong?* as I located pieces of the scalp on the back wall, ceiling, curtains and even on the carpet in front of him. It was everywhere. Before long, I found myself balancing with both feet on the arms of a recliner, stretch out to reach the top of the curtain rod to retrieve a biscuit-sized piece of skull. This piece had bloody hair on one side, still glistening wet, and remnants of brain fused to the skull on the other side. The brain was hanging off the bone like dangling minced meat. As the officers looked on in awe, I knew they had never seen anything like this also.

As we closed the final zip-lock bag, the officers asked if we would be taking the rifle with us. Looking somewhat confused, I informed them that I didn't think it would be a good idea as neither of us had a gun licence.[†]

It is possible the police had thought the coroner might require it, or that there might be fragments of brain and skull on the rifle that would have to be removed. I'm still unsure, but we left the gun at the scene for the police to deal with.

On leaving the scene that night, I knew it would impact all who witnessed it. I couldn't comprehend what would drive someone to carry out such a desperate act. The image I encountered that day, walking into that lounge room stained with blood and the man's missing scalp, has been etched in my memory. Unlike the blood on the wall, this vision cannot be washed away.

[†]In Australia, new gun laws had just been introduced. This was in response to a gunman killing 35 people in Port Arthur, Tasmania, four years prior.

THE BACKSTORY

Lying awake under the covers, Basil popped his head out like an animal in its burrow to see the morning sun glowing softly from behind heavy, closed curtains. The failure of the drapes to darken the room completely disappointed Basil, as he did not want the morning to come. *Judging by the light, it's about 9 am*, he thought, *maybe 9:45*. Not having work to go to after being laid off from his job and after months of rejections from many job applications, he'd all but given up. Now, his only enjoyment came from playing a game he invented just for himself – judging what time it was when he opened his eyes. The nights were long. Basil found it difficult to sleep and knew all too well that time slows down just past 1 am.

Basil did not want to part with his warm comfy bed, and, as he had no real reason to get up, he stayed there. Just like every other morning, he pondered life's disappointments and allowed the thick fog to cloud his mind. In his depressive state, he vaguely remembered when life was fun and carefree: the excitement of catching up with friends, socialising at the pub, driving down to the beach and mucking around in the surf. It was like these old distant memories were from another life. Now all that remained was a constant numbness throughout his entire body.

Finally, as his bladder woke up and beckoned him to relieve himself, the urge to get up was far stronger than the comfort of his warm cocoon-like sheets. Walking to the bathroom was like trudging through quicksand, and he struggled even to stand upright. After making a cup of coffee, the lingering empty feeling surrounding him became unbearable, so he walked over to the television and switched it on. Like an old mate keeping him company, the voices on the television were familiar and reliable. However, on this morning flicking through the channels, he found nothing remotely interesting — even the comedy channel had lost all humour. It felt like walking into a pub only to discover that all your mates had given up drinking months ago.

Contemplating his own Groundhog Day, today being just like yesterday and the day before that and all the other days for a month, Basil could not see any light at the end of the tunnel. He sat there, in the armchair, contemplating his existence. *Would anyone miss me if I wasn't here? Would anyone even care enough to notice I was gone?*

For each question, Basil couldn't fathom an answer that satisfied him. Questioning his existence ignited a spark, and he began to accept his invisibility. The spark quickly became a small flame. Basil could feel the dark black hole inside him grow more expansive with every thought. The pain of trying to charge an old battery that no longer held any charge was now like a medieval iron chair with its hundreds of sharp-pointed nails penetrating every inch of his body. He has a sudden, decisive thought: *I'm gonna end this misery today!* The tiny flame erupted into a scorching blaze inside his head: today would be execution day.

Suddenly, today had meaning. Today was going to be different to all the other days. Today had a purpose.

Just the thought of relieving the pain was like a jailbreak from his own fortress prison. *Time to get to work,* he thought.

Basil remembered the old 22-millimetre rifle in the top of the back cupboard that his friends used to call 'the broomstick'. They used it to shoot rabbits down at the old farmhouse. He remembered the fun times they had, driving around the paddocks and along channel banks with the spotlight hooked up to the front of the ute. One mate would be driving and another would hold a second spotlight out of the passenger side window, scanning for foxes and rabbits. A few mates would be on the back of the ute to call out when something was spotted, and would then point the rifle at the intended target before pulling the trigger. Cheers would go up if they hit the target; otherwise, words of encouragement for next time were offered if the prey got away. The night's catch would be hung up overnight and cleaned the next day. The smell of the rabbits being cleaned overcame his nostrils for a moment. Half a smile flickered on one side of his mouth when he remembered the time his mate, Bob, shot his left foot in a hunting accident. From then on, everyone called him Lefty.

As quickly as the smile came, it disappeared. Basil headed to the cupboard and reached behind all the junk accumulated over time to retrieve the rifle. Holding the 'old broomstick' in his hands felt like a ticket … to a final destination.

Basil took just one copper bullet out of the box and securely lodged it in its place within the magazine. He clipped the magazine back to the gun. He then plucked back the bolt with the palm of his hands in one motion. Tilting the gun to one side, he performed a final check to make sure everything is secure. He headed to the lounge room. The strength in his legs began to weaken, but his desire to end this misery did not. He sat back down in his armchair. He didn't want to drag this out. He had made up his mind; this was not going to be another thing he failed at.

Sitting in a mesmerised state, Basil held the rifle up, turned it to face him and looked down its barrel. He reasoned with the tip of the gun before placing the end in his mouth. The cold metallic taste landed on his tongue. His right index finger began to flirt with the trigger, slowly caressing the edges. He began to apply pressure to the trigger. All he needed now was for the trigger to move half a centimetre. Like a starter's pistol being fired after the call: *Ready, Set, …*

The deafening sound of the black dog howling rings in his ears for the last time.

In Closing: Condemned

*"You can be a king or a street sweeper, but
everyone dances with the Grim Reaper."*
Robert Alton Harris

"Life is too short." This saying has been repeated many times in passive conversations when expressing our time alive. On the rugged road of life, we often forget to appreciate how short life is.

Some years after I had walked away from being an undertaker, I found myself in a room filled with strangers for a business meeting. One presenter spoke about the importance of living life to the fullest and how little time we have. He used an example that has stuck in my mind to this very day. It resonated with me in a way that made me reflect on my existence and my purpose in life. It was like someone spoke just enough of the right words to turn a key in my mind, like a bank volt that had just been cracked.

During the exercise, we were asked to draw 100 little boxes. I was standing up at the time and, with pen and paper in hand, I awkwardly drew 100 little boxes. We were then asked to shade in the boxes for each year we celebrated a birthday. Some people in the room took longer to complete this task than others. As I was one of the few younger people in the room, I shaded 32 boxes. I was feeling quite silly colouring, in as if I was in grade 2 again, but I was also curious to know where this was going. Everyone busily coloured their boxes while making age-related jokes to the people sitting next to them. The mood in the room lightened as people who didn't know each other moments ago chuckled to each other.

When everyone had finished scribbling away, the presenter continued. He informed us of the life expectancy at the time for men and women, which from memory was 69 years for men and 71.1 years for women. He instructed us to put a cross in the box to represent this life expectancy. I put a cross in the 69th box. Then, like a bomb had been dropped in the room, everyone's faces began to show the signs of an epiphany: a sudden realisation of just how short life is. Looking around, I could see people peering deep into their pieces of paper, mesmerised by the unshaded boxes. Their minds ticked as they calculated how many more years they had left. We were given a glimpse through a crack in the door of destiny.

I looked at my unshaded boxes and at the reactions throughout the room. I was aware that the number of boxes I had left unshaded was far greater than that of many people in the room. I still had time to adapt, grow, live and play after learning to view life from this new perspective. The look on the faces of some people in the room was despair. But the presenter had not finished with his example. He continued.

'Who knows of someone who suffered from cancer and died?' he asked.

Nearly everyone's hand went up. Some then shared their stories. A couple of people even spoke of their own battles with cancer. The presenter made his point that not everyone gets the luxury to live to the life expectancy. In other words, the time we think we have could dramatically be reduced.

This led him to his point, which was to enjoy life and appreciate our moments. He emphasised how we mustn't make life all about work but live, laugh and love. Walking away that day, I saw life in a new light. I've tried to live my life accordingly ever since.

My journey as an undertaker, in a world I knew little about, had taught me so much by the time I decided to walk away. Of all the lessons I learnt as an undertaker, the harshest was that life is as fragile as thin ice forming on a lake; it can easily be broken. I now view my experiences as a privilege, as they have given me greater appreciation for everything else in my life. Like waking from a daydream – or in my case, someone else's nightmare — I have been given an insight into a hidden world just below the surface of everyday life. I have used these experiences to reflect on my own life. When some encounters, events, or circumstances seem bad, I know first-hand that life can always get worse in a split second. I hope my experiences will have the same impact on the reader's life — your life — and remind you to appreciate the gift of life and use this knowledge to achieve your own awakening.

While working as an undertaker, I often wondered what kind of life the deceased people I encountered had lived. I would then wonder about my own life. I have heard the phrase that the truth is 'We're all slowly dying', and therefore, we should live our life to its potential; however, the reality is that most people are limited to what they think they can do in life. I have been accused of having a lust for life. People who know me know I am not afraid to take up a challenge. Many people will have 'analysis paralysis' before committing to anything. A driving characteristic of most entrepreneurs is that they jump straight into the unknown with complete faith in their capabilities. Sure, there is some consideration of the risks and a lot of hard work involved. Seneca said:

> *"It is not because things are difficult that we do not dare.*
> *It is because we do not dare those things are difficult."*

This is how I choose to live.

Daily, we are surrounded by death. Death can come to us anywhere at any time. It is said that we are less than a metre away from death every day. Every second, 1.8 people die. On the bright side, 4.2 humans are born on average every second. My biggest concern is that one day I will be on my death bed harbouring regret – regretting not taking the opportunities life has offered me.

The most expensive real estate is in cemeteries because many people die with regret. They did not take the opportunities and ideas that life presented to them. Some of the world's most incredible concepts have come to people like a flash while they are in bed about to fall asleep, or while working on a completely different project, or even while driving. We have to be aware enough to be more aware of these concepts and grab hold of them when they come to us. The late Michael Jackson was known to get up in the middle of the night to write down ideas that struck him like a freak bolt of lightning. He knew that if he did not write them down, they would be gone by morning.

In my own flash of inspiration, I knew I needed to write down the stories I encountered as an undertaker. At first, I was hesitant. I was mortified of being wrong or embarrassed by what people may think, especially as I hadn't written anything like it before. In the end, I imagined myself on my death bed, wondering what could have been. I was more petrified by doing nothing.

It's amazing that in a world full of people – 7.9 billion to be exact (at the time of writing) – every one of those people will face death at some point. Even if they try to cheat death, death will always have its own plan, like a game of jeopardy.

I've not seen what lies beyond this world. Maybe when we all make the journey to the afterlife, it will be revealed to us that all the gods and heaven and the devils and hell exist inside us while we experience this short thing called life.

Life can be seen to be filled with endless opportunities. I hope you can live your life to its full potential.

RONNY ALLARD